# RESURRECTED BUMPKIN

## SAM CHEEVER

ELECTRIC PROSE PUBLICATIONS

*Meanwhile, in a local support group for people with control issues...*

Hi! I'm Joey, and I'm learning to cope with not having control over *any* aspect of my life.

Really, I am.

So what if my boyfriend's parents are here for a visit. I can deal with that, right? They probably won't *completely* hate me. I'm sure they won't judge me for being an unrepentant bumpkin.

Oh, and somebody's trying to kill my mom. There's no way that can end badly.

But, surely I can find the villain before he accomplishes his deadly task, right?

At least Hal's parents are here to watch me completely melt down and lose my mind. Sooo, that's cool.

Sigh... Stick a pitchfork in me. I'm dung.

# 1

---

I stared at the television, riveted on the scene as the cameras skimmed over the dark, gated mansion that had once belonged to Garland Medford. The news crew apparently hadn't been invited past the gate because the figure strolling across the grounds was too far away to really identify from the tape.

He was a big guy, with sandy brown hair that was too long on his neck. He was wearing a suit that looked tailor-made for his long, heavy body.

"Public documents state that Gil Christopher gained a controlling interest in Garland Medford's successful corporation upon his boss' death," said the plastic-faced blonde reporter behind the microphone. "Speculation is rife over whether Medford's long-time right-hand man would continue the questionable business practices attributed to his boss, but he does seem to be treating the spectacular mansion the same way Medford did, as both residence and business hub."

My cell phone buzzed against the granite countertop. Not taking my eyes off the small TV across the room, I blindly reached for it.

"Gil Christopher is by all accounts a calculating, unscrupulous man who's been investigated multiple times by the FBI. Unfortunately, the feds have not been able to make any charges stick on an array of crimes that are alleged to include money laundering, blackmail, and influence peddling. There's even speculation his crimes might include kidnapping and human trafficking. It seems..." said barbie with a mic, "...there's little doubt that Garland Medford's right-hand man is continuing with business as usual in the wake of his boss's suspicious death."

I tore my eyes away from the screen to look at the ID on my cell. It was an unknown number. I briefly considered not answering the call, but...yeah, Pavlov could have performed his little experiment on me just as well as the dogs and gotten the same result. *Joey hears a phone ring. Joey feels compelled to answer said phone.* I couldn't seem to help myself. "Hello?"

"Joey? How are you, sweetie? I haven't heard your voice in ages."

My lips curved up in an instant grin. "Mom! Hi!

I've missed you. I'm great. How are you? And Dev?" I no longer called him Uncle Dev, the name too reminiscent of a painful time in my life.

"I'm great. Dev is...well." She paused long enough to make me frown.

"Has something happened?"

"No. Don't be silly."

There was something in her voice. Something uncomfortable. And when she spoke again, her tone was filled with forced lightness. "Devon's fine. He and I are just having a spat. It'll pass." She expelled a soft sigh, the sound barely carrying through the phone line. "I don't want to talk about that. I'm calling with good news."

"Oh?" I tried really hard not to let concern fill my voice. Thinking about my mom had become a constant exercise in worry. She'd been in danger longer than I knew since I'd thought she was dead for the first couple of years. And once I'd learned she wasn't, I'd realized that could change in the blink of an eye if a certain bad element learned she was still alive. Worrying about her was a hard habit to shake. I hadn't accomplished it in any meaningful way. I had moments...hours...when my life drew my mind away from thoughts of her plight.

But I always came back to it sooner rather than later.

The only exception had been a wonderful few

days two Christmases ago when she and Dev had made a surprise visit. Those two days had been filled with happiness in seeing them again. They'd been days of love and laughter. They'd been too few when compared to the span of worry-filled days before and after. But they'd been a gift I'd cherished none-the-less.

"...coming to see you."

I blinked, realizing my wool-gathering had caused me to miss her words. Surely I hadn't heard what I'd thought I'd heard. "What?"

She laughed, the sound slightly brittle. "I said, I'm coming to see you. I can't wait, honey. We have so much to catch up on."

I wanted to be thrilled. I wanted to pretend it would be a normal visit. I wanted to laugh with her and make plans for her trip.

But there was that one pesky problem—her imminent death.

"It's not safe, Mom."

"Pshaw! You sound like Devon." Her tone was definitely bitter that time. "I'm sick to death of hiding. I want to see you. I want to see that hand-some boyfriend of yours and your adorable fur babies. Just for a couple of days, I want to be normal."

My heart broke at the longing in her voice. Since my thoughts had mirrored hers, I couldn't exactly blame her.

"Garland Medford is gone, Joey. I can't hide out here forever. I need to pick my life back up and move on."

"Yes, he's gone. But his organization is still in place. It's not safe yet."

"You don't want me to come?" Her tone had gone from wistful to angry in a blink.

"Of course I want you to come. There's nothing I'd like more than that. Mom..." I chewed my lip, trying to think of something that would impress upon her how much I missed her, without giving her additional reasons to come. "I'm scared." I hadn't meant for the words to come out sounding so pathetic. But they had.

I could almost hear her heart breaking through the line.

"Oh, honey."

Tears slid down my cheeks, plopping onto my bare feet. Caphy rose from her comfy dog bed and trotted over, leaning against my leg and whining softly.

I reached down and scratched behind her ears to reassure her.

"I'll be there soon, Joey. I love you, sweetie."

"Wait, mom..."

The connection was gone.

"Dangit!" I exclaimed. I'd totally messed that up. I was such a dope.

Sighing, I dropped my cell on the counter and

leaned my elbows on the cool granite, burying my face in my hands.

Caphy lay her squishy head on my feet, heaving a sigh. Her warmth reminded me I needed to put on some socks. The temps outside were frigid, and the tile floor was cold.

My phone rang with Hal's ringtone. I debated not answering. He'd hear the tears in my voice and want to come over. I wasn't sure I felt like seeing anyone at that moment.

My mom was coming to see me. The joyful spark in my chest at the thought was impossible to squelch. I *had* missed her. So badly. A tiny part of me had hoped she would show up to surprise me the previous month at Christmas.

She hadn't. I'd worked hard not to let it ruin our wonderful Christmas together. Hal had gone out of his way to make it the best. The weather had cooperated, giving us eight sparkling inches of snow to help create the perfect holiday. We'd done the whole snowman, snow-ball fight, roaring fire, and hot chocolate with little baby marshmallows thing. It had been a storybook day.

Nearly perfect.

Nearly.

Only one thing had marred the holidays for me. And that one thing was about to make an appearance. I should be delighted. I *was* happy. But I was worried too. And feeling slightly guilty that I was glad she was coming despite the danger.

I grabbed my cell just before it would have gone to voicemail. "Hey," I said to Hal.

Silence met my greeting. Voices sounded in the background, accompanied by the sound of dishes clanking together. "Hal?"

"Hello, Joey."

I blinked in surprise. The voice didn't belong to my boyfriend. "Who is this?"

Silence. The connection died, the background sounds sliced away. I quickly redialed, my mind playing the sound of that voice over and over again as I tried to identify it.

I couldn't shake the notion that it was familiar.

The call connected, dragging my pulse up with every unanswered ring. I hung up and dialed again. "Come on, come on, come on..."

"Hello?"

*Oh, thank goodness.* "Hal!"

"Hey, honey." His tone went from startled at my overly exuberant greeting to concern. "What's wrong?"

I took a deep breath and eased it out through my lips. "I was so worried."

There was a jangling sound, like a shop door bell. "Tell me what's happening."

"No!" I paused to reel myself in. "I mean, there's no need. I'm fine. I was worried about you."

"Me? Why?"

"Who was the guy who just called me on your phone?"

Silence again. "That would be me."

"No. my phone rang a couple of minutes ago. Somebody else was on your cell."

More silence. "That's not possible, honey."

"I'm telling you, the call had your ringtone. It was your phone. Is it possible somebody picked it up and you didn't notice?"

"No, I..." He swore softly. "This kid ran into me and spilled my coffee all over him. I was arguing with him for a minute. I ended up ordering him a coffee to calm him down."

"Where was your phone during all this?"

"It was..." He sighed. "It was on the table. But the caller would have to be someone who knows you. Did you recognize the voice?"

*Yes!* I thought in frustration. *But I don't know who it was.* "I couldn't place it, no. Hal, what are the chances someone who knows me and my relationship with you would just happen to be nearby when you briefly abandoned your phone?"

"Not good. Someone was clearly trying to spook you."

*But why?* I asked myself. *And why now?*

"I'm on my way. We need to figure this out. I don't like it at all."

"See you soon." I disconnected and looked at Caphy, a chill sliding down my spine. I agreed with Hal. I didn't like it either.

Especially with my mother planning to show up at my house.

# 2

---

Too antsy to check email or pay the bills that were waiting for me on the counter, I was folding laundry on the big island that dominated my kitchen. Ethel Squeaks tottered into the kitchen, pushing her red ball in front of her. Caphy looked up from her spot at my feet but didn't try to steal the ball from the pig, not even after Ethel rolled it closer in an obvious attempt to get her to play.

My phone rang and I jumped at the sound, the general ringtone telling me it wasn't one of my close friends. I didn't recognize the number on the screen, but curiosity made me answer the phone anyway. Pavlov's Joey, remember? "Hello?"

"Joey?"

The familiar voice allowed the knot in my belly to loosen. "Hey, Dev. How are you?"

"I'm fine. But I'm worried about your mother."

And, just like that, the knot cranked tighter again. "Why? What's happened?"

"She's gone."

"What do you mean, she's gone? Where did she go?"

"If I knew that, I'd go get her, Joey. We had words, and I left to cool off. When I got back to the place where we're staying, she was gone. Her suitcase is gone too. And most of her clothes. I'm worried, Joey."

I chewed my lip, knowing that I should tell him about my mother calling earlier. But something kept the words from marching past my lips. If my mom had wanted Dev to know, wouldn't she have told him? "Has she said anything about going anywhere?" I was hoping he'd tell me she'd talked about visiting me, so I'd know it was okay to tell him.

"Not a word. She's been restless lately. Unhappy. It's why we fought. She's been short with me for days. I've felt as if she was hiding something. So, I confronted her about it."

"What would she be hiding from you?"

"I wish I knew, Joey. She won't tell me. In fact, she denies even being unhappy. I was hoping that maybe she called you?"

Guilt ate a hole in my belly. Devon hadn't always been honest with me, but I was pretty sure he'd always had my mother's best interests at heart. In fact, he was probably the biggest reason she was still alive. I sighed. "Look, Dev, she did call me. She's okay."

"Where is she?" He sounded so desperate, I really wished I could tell him. "I don't know. I assumed she was still with you." That wasn't a lie, at least.

"You're sure? She didn't tell you where she was going?"

I panicked. Answering *that* question would put me directly into lie territory. "We didn't talk for long. She seemed excited about something, but she didn't tell me what. I can honestly say, I don't know what she's up to."

I chewed my bottom lip, doubt making me sick to my stomach. I should just tell him she was coming to Deer Hollow. He'd be really mad when he found out. She was putting herself into danger and I was allowing it to happen.

"Okay. If you hear from her again, will you let me know?"

"I will." That was an easier promise to make since I fully intended to make my mom call him when she got to Deer Hollow. "Take care of yourself," I told the man who'd been my dad's best friend for his whole life. "Try not to worry. Mom's a free spirit, but she's not reckless." Not much anyway. "I'm sure she's keeping herself safe."

A beat of silence told me he wasn't buying it. "I'll talk to you soon, Joey."

He hung up before I got a chance to say goodbye. Was it my guilt talking to me? Or had he been cooler to me at the end than he'd been at the start of the phone call?

I shoved my phone away and hid my face in my hands, suddenly so tired. How was it possible to be so tired when I wasn't even thirty years old yet?

Caphy suddenly jumped to her feet and barked. A moment later, the front door closed with a decisive snap.

"Joey?"

"In the kitchen."

Hal came through the door with Caphy dancing by his side and Ethel trotting along behind him. As he wrapped me in a welcome hug, the red ball slowly eased in behind him, lightly booping against the back of his shoe and stopping.

He reached down and grabbed the ball, tossing it through the kitchen door before turning to me.

Both animals surged out of the room after the ball.

"I've been wracking my brain on the drive over here," Hal said, dropping onto a stool at the island. "I've decided that whoever it was has been watching me enough to know my habits."

Hal had started doing work for the Amity Investigative business at the *Bend Over and Coffee* shop in town on Mondays and Fridays because the Internet connection was better there than at either my house or his little cabin deep in the woods.

If someone had been paying attention, they might have noticed.

"Okay," I agreed. "That's plausible. But why? And who?"

He shook his head. "No idea. I didn't notice anyone skulking around. And more importantly, unless my whole encounter with that guy who bumped into me was just a lucky happenstance for my stalker, it had to have been someone with the means and interest in bribing the guy to get what he wanted."

"We need to find the guy who bumped into you."

He nodded. "Already thought of that. He was gone by the time I talked to you. But I'm pretty sure I've seen him in the shop before."

The *Bend Over and Coffee* was a new shop in Deer Hollow. One of several that had popped up after two new subdivisions expanded the population of our little town by three times what it had been before the new construction. The Deer Hollow gossip mill was abuzz about the owner, who was apparently the wife of a new proctologist in town. Thus the strange name, which had been a stroke of genius since the funny name got people into the place, and the delicious pastries and rich, steamy coffee kept them coming back.

"Hopefully, he'll be able to tell us who paid him to distract you. Or at least give us a description."

Hal nodded, tugging his cell from his pocket when it rang. "Hello?" His eyes widened. "Oh, hey..." Whoever was on the other end of the line must have cut him off mid-sentence. He frowned. "Okay, sure. Can you tell me what this is about?"

I motioned toward the coffee machine, and he nodded. As I set about making us both cups of coffee, he finished up the very one-sided conversation.

"Who was that?" I asked, handing him his coffee.

"Cal." He sipped, making a happy face. "Thanks. That tastes great. Between the guy bumping into me and pitching a fit, and then you scaring the hash browns out of me, I never did get to drink my coffee."

I slid onto a stool next to him. "What's Cal up to?" Cal was Hal's brother and the other half of their company, Amity Investigations. He was also dating my favorite and, well, only cousin, Felicity Chance, the city mouse to my country rodent.

"He's coming to Deer Hollow."

My eyes went wide over the coffee mug. "Seriously? Has the world ended?"

Hal laughed. "No. He says he's following up on something and the trail is leading him here. He's bringing Felly. They're hoping we'll have dinner with them." He grinned. "She said to tell you there'd better be banana cream pie left."

I grinned back. "Fun!" having Felly in Deer Hollow was like an answer to a prayer. Not only would she distract me from my worries about my mom. But she and I made a pretty good team figuring things out. Maybe she could help me decide what to do about my mom apparently losing her ever-loving mind. "How long will they be staying?"

"Cal was vague, but at least a couple of nights. He asked me to help him look for someone."

I hid my grin. With the boys away, the city and country mice could play. Any way you sliced that cheese, problems were about to be solved.

Hal pulled out his phone and dialed a number. "Hi, is this Kelly?" He smiled. "Hey, Kelly. It's Hal Amity. I was wondering if you could help me with something."

I listened as Hal told the owner of the coffee shop about the phone call to me and asked her if she knew the guy he'd had his little altercation with. He grabbed my grocery list and tore the front sheet of paper off, jotting down a name and number. "Great. Thanks so much."

Hal ended the call and looked at me. "I'm going to ask Arno to contact this guy and see if he can get him to fess up about the not-so-accidental bumpage at the coffee shop."

I nodded, thinking he was very good at being a

Private Investigator. And pretty much everything else he tried.

Leaving him to talk to Arno, I went upstairs to tidy up the guest rooms for Felly and my mom.

---

I glanced at my cell again, checking the time. "They're late. Are you sure they wanted to meet here?"

Hal gave me a patient smile. "My response hasn't changed from the last five times you've asked that question."

I deflated, feeling guilty. "Sorry. It's just not like Felly to be late."

"Cal might have been late getting out of the office. Fridays can be a bit hairy there. Everybody seems to think they can hire a PI on Friday afternoon to have somebody followed on Saturday morning." He shook his dark head, seemingly disgusted with the human race. But a smile twitched on his lips. "Or, maybe Felly had trouble picking out the right purse for the visit."

I smacked him on the arm. "Neanderthal!"

He chuckled warmly, snaking an arm over the back of the booth and tugging me close. "Have I ever told you you're cute when you're annoyed?"

"No. But that means I'm probably adorable most of the time we're together."

He hissed, wincing. "Ouch."

A horn blared from the curb, and my gaze jerked around to find my cousin hopping out of her boyfriend's big truck before he could come around to open the door for her. She waved excitedly when she spotted us through the window, then promptly tripped over a crack in the sidewalk and stumbled toward us, arms windmilling and beaded alligator purse swinging in a deadly arc as she tried to regain her balance.

Looking like he was accustomed to seeing his girlfriend flailing away, Cal calmly reached out and grabbed one slender arm, tugging her to an ordered stop. He shifted away from the attack-purse and snagged it in one big hand before it could clock him in the head.

Felly's lips curved in what I recognized as an embarrassed laugh, judging by the fresh pink in her cheeks. Cal grinned back at her, then tugged her in for a quick kiss.

"Now, that's adorable," I told Hal.

He blew air through his lips, but I could tell he was pleased to see his brother happy.

Hal slid from the booth as his brother opened the door to Sonny's Diner. I slid out behind him, running to greet Felly with a squeal that made heads all through the diner turn in our direction. "I'm so glad to see you!" I threw myself into her arms, and she squealed too. Unfortunately, her squeal was one of alarm as I overbalanced us, and she fell into the door. Our combined weight shoved the door open again, and there was a soft grunt as it smacked into a large body trying to enter the diner behind Felly and Cal.

With only the merest tightening around his Sapphire blue eyes, Cal reached out and snagged one of Felly's arms, gently tugging us both away from the door.

A heavyset man in a well-worn flannel shirt came through the door, glaring at me. "Sorry, Bobo." I gave him a sheepish smile as he shook his head.

"Let me guess, this girl's related to you?" he asked.

The smile felt tight on my lips. "How'd you know?"

"She shares the same graceful demeanor." Bobo Biddens was a local farmer whose real name was Pete, but everybody called him Bobo because his last name was reminiscent of a hobbit's. That, and his propensity for dual breakfasts and over-achieving hair follicles on his big feet pretty much ensured he'd evermore be Deer Hollow's Hobbit in residence.

"Very funny," I told the big man as he chuckled. He nodded at Cal and then did a double-take as he spotted Hal. "Oh," said Bobo. "I thought you were..." He scanned a look between the two brothers, an understanding light slowly filling his eyes. "You must be twins."

Cal offered Bobo a hand. "Cal Amity. It's nice to meet you."

Bobo shook his hand and nodded at Hal before lumbering toward his usual spot at the counter. He dropped onto a spinning stool and turned to me, poking two fingers in a vee toward his eyes and then toward the pie cooler behind the counter.

I bristled, shooting Max a panicked look. She saw me and shook her head. "Already put some back," she called across the busy diner.

I relaxed and returned the "I'll be watching you" gesture to Bobo.

He chuckled good-naturedly.

We sat down. Max came over with her order pad, sliding two glasses of water in front of Felly and Cal. "I didn't know you had a twin, Hal."

Hal smiled at her. "You think he looks like me?"

Max laughed as if she thought he was joking. To her eye, they were clearly twins.

Except they weren't. Cal was actually ten months older than Hal and had blue eyes to Hal's forest green ones, but they certainly looked enough alike to pass. Both men had hair that was black enough to give off blue highlights in the right lighting, and both wore it longish, the thick, slightly wavy pelts swept back from well-formed, masculine faces. Both had dense black lashes that would make any woman besotted as well as jealous. Both men were over six feet tall, but seeing them side by side, I realized Hal was an inch taller than his older brother. Both men were strongly built and had perfect Greek noses above lushly-formed mouths. Though, I noticed Cal's bottom lip was maybe a skosh fuller than Hal's.

"I'll be back in a few to take your orders."

Tucking a long, wavy strand of light brown hair behind one ear. Felly reached across the table and squeezed my hand. "I'm so happy to be here." The sparkle in her turquoise eyes proved the truth in her words.

I couldn't help grinning back. "I can't remember when we saw each other last."

"It was last March," Felly said. "For that wine tasting thing."

Ah, yes. How could I forget? We'd gone to Felly's favorite local winery in Indianapolis and had worked our way through most of the available inventory. Then we'd staggered to a nearby hotel rather than climb back into my Jeep and endanger the driving public around Indy.

The rest of the night was fuzzy in my memory, but I had a vague and shadowy recollection of wearing a bed sheet and chanting, "Toga, toga, toga" while dancing the chicken dance with open bottles of wine in our hands.

The hangover the next morning had been monumental, and I'd sworn never to go to another wine tasting with my cousin.

I'd meant it with every fiber of my wine-satu-rated being.

"That was so much fun," Felly said. "We should do it again."

"Absolutely!" my traitorous lips said before my brain had time to object.

"Judging by the look on your face," Hal said, grinning, "I need details."

Felly shook her head. "What happens at the post-wine-tasting toga party, stays at the post-wine-tasting toga party."

Cal's eyes widened. "Now *I'm* intrigued. You know you're going to have to spill."

Felly held the beaded alligator monstrosity up between them. "Talk to the alligator."

I snorted out a laugh.

"Nice purse," Max said, eying Felly's treasure.

Felly's eyes sparkled with pleasure. "I know, right?"

"Where'd you get it?"

Felly sighed. "Bilksville, Alabama." She sighed, looking misty-eyed. "Good times."

"She brought me back a frog clutch," I told Max with a grin.

Felly laughed. "So cute." She nudged Cal in the arm. "We need to go back sometime."

He shook his head. "Unless Lena Borne can make them from jail, I doubt there will be any more beaded reptile purses."

She deflated, pouting. "Such a shame."

"Jail?" Max asked, her dark brows lifting. "Do tell."

"Long story," Felly said with a grin.

Sensing she wasn't going to hear it, Max nodded. "What are you folks havin' tonight?"

"Aside from banana cream pie?" I said with a look toward the mountain sitting at the counter. As if sensing my gaze burning through his flannel, Bobo turned and winked.

Max rolled her eyes. "Your slices are safe. Are you having dinner? Or just dessert?"

I was tempted to say just dessert, but the Greek god and his brother, the Greek deity, were giving me the "you have to eat your vegetables before you have dessert" look.

"I'll have the pork chop dinner," I told Max.

"Me too," Felly agreed. The look she threw me was clear. We were just getting dinner over with, so we could get to the good stuff. We shared a knowing smile. Felicity Chance and I were cousins, but our family connection was only the smallest part of why we loved each other. We'd have been best friends even if we weren't related. We shared a love of mystery-solving; tall, dark, and handsome men; and a lifelong passion for sweets and carbs.

That she had nary an inch of extra flesh on her svelte, five-foot-five-inch frame was the only bug in the ointment of our mutual admiration.

I would admit that my bumpkin eating ways had added curves to my five-foot-four-inch physique. I'd have to step up my walks with Caphy to offset the calories because there was no way I was giving up pie.

The two immortals ordered vegetable omelets and dry wheat toast, earning dual scowls from the less persnickety eaters at the table.

They didn't even seem to notice. "Tell us about this case that brings you to Deer Hollow," Hal said to his brother. "I wasn't aware of any cases with a connection."

Cal nodded, wiping his lips after taking a long drink of water. "This is something new." His gaze slid to me, and I got the distinct impression he didn't want to talk in front of me.

I zipped my lips. "I won't spill. Hal and I work on cases together all the time."

Cal sighed. "It's not that. I trust you as much as I trust Hal." He frowned, his long, perfectly-manicured fingers shoving at his water-spotted utensils.

Yet he wouldn't tell me.

"What?" I scowled at him. "Tell me, Cal. Whatever it is, it's better if I know."

When he still hesitated, Hal said, "She's right, bro. Tell us."

Cal's gaze lifted to his brother's, hesitated, and then swung to me. "It's Garland Medford. We think he might still be alive."

## 3

I'd had a strong suspicion that Medford was alive, but hearing the words still shocked me to stillness. The previous summer, after we'd closed a drugs and murder case that Hal's and Cal's younger brother, Asher, brought to our doorstep, I'd found a note in my mailbox that made me wonder if the wealthy businessman slash all-around bad guy might still be among the living.

It had been a single sentence, typed across a folded piece of paper. But it had caused my world to tilt on its axis.

*Reports of my demise are greatly exaggerated. G*

I was dimly aware of voices around me, but my mind was swirling with the knowledge that he was alive. And my mother was coming to Deer Hollow.

"No!"

I didn't realize I'd spoken the word aloud until

the conversation around me sliced off with the violence of a verbal guillotine.

"Joey?" Hal said, leaning closer. "Are you okay, honey?"

I turned to him, my expression no doubt filled with stark terror. "My mom."

He held my gaze for a beat and then his hand clasped mine, enveloping it in soothing warmth. He looked at Cal. "You know about the history between Medford and Joey's parents?"

Cal nodded, his expression telling me he knew where his brother was going with the question. "It's why I'm here. I have no reason to believe that Garland Medford is here in Deer Hollow. I'm just being cautious. I thought Hal and I could sniff around a bit. See if there's any sign of him."

I relaxed at the meaning behind his words. Cal was offering his services to help protect my family from Medford. I smiled, tears burning in my eyes. "Thank you."

Cal smiled back. "No worries. I've missed this big ape anyway. It's been a while since I've seen him." Cal looked away, his gorgeous eyes shifting with something that looked like guilt. "I feel bad I wasn't around to help with the whole Asher thing."

Hal's dark brows arched. "Are you?"

To my surprise, Cal's lips twitched in a smile he wouldn't let loose. "A little bit."

The two brothers stared at each other across the table, indulging in some kind of silent communication built during years of living and working together and a general instinct for how each other's mind worked.

"Here we go," Max said, breaking the silence at our table. "Two delicious pork chop dinners." She placed the steaming plates, laden with a massive grilled pork chop, a generous mound of garlic mashed potatoes, and healthy portions of buttered corn in front of Felly and me. Max looked down at the remaining omelets in her hands and grimaced. "And two healthy omelets with no butter, no guilt, and no flavor."

Without looking up from my plate, I lifted a hand into the air and Max slapped it. "Enjoy your meals, *girls*."

The emphasis she put on the word "girls" made me wonder if she was trying to call the gods sissies for ordering chick food. But maybe I was over-thinking it. She probably just knew that, of the four of us, Felly and I would be the only ones enjoying our food.

"They don't pull any punches around here, do they?" Cal asked, watching Max saunter away with a cocky sway to her hips.

"Not even a little bit," Hal agreed, taking a bite of his omelet and glancing longingly toward the salt and pepper shakers.

I grinned. I'd corrupt him eventually. It was only a matter of time.

"Mmmmmm," Felly and I said in unison, our eyes rolling back in our heads.

Okay, maybe it wouldn't be such a hardship to eat my real food before dessert. I grinned around my mouthful of creamy potatoes.

"Tell us about Medford," Hal pressed. "Has he been seen? Why do you think he's alive?"

"He hasn't been sighted, no."

My worry eased a little when I heard that. Maybe Cal was wrong after all. Maybe Garland Medford hadn't returned from the grave.

*Reports of my demise are greatly exaggerated. G*

I shook my head as if to dispel the spot on my brain where those words had been burned like a brand.

"Things are happening in his organization," Cal said. "There have been a couple of 'accidental' deaths lately. People who you'd probably consider loose ends if you were Medford."

"People who could give the feds information about his organization that he wouldn't want to be shared?" Hal asked.

Cal nodded, shoving his empty plate away. "The activity tells me that one of two things is happening. Either Medford's back and he's planning Evil World Domination Take 2..."

"Or someone is taking over his operation," Hal finished for his brother.

"Yeah." Cal took a moment to wipe his lips. "I'm leaning toward option one."

"Why?" I asked because I was curious.

"Medford ruled his organization with an iron fist. He ran a totally centralized op with him and one other guy as the repositories of all key information. Rule number 1, nothing was done without a direct order from Medford or Christopher. Anybody who broke that rule ran smack into Rule number 2."

"Which was?" Hal asked.

"No second chances." Cal shook his head. "Even his second didn't so much as flick dandruff off a competitor's shoulder without checking with Medford first."

"That sounds stressful," Felly said, pushing her empty plate away with a dainty burp.

"Yes. It does," Cal agreed, frowning.

"What happened with the second?" Hal asked. "After the accident that supposedly took out his boss?"

"He went underground for a while," Cal told them. "Rumors were that he feared he was next on the list."

"And now?" Felly asked, seemingly very interested in the story Cal was telling. I sometimes forgot that my cousin was every bit as much of a mystery buff as I was. I'd heard she'd gotten into quite a bit of hot water over her exploits down south, trying to find her miscreant father.

"That's what's got my antennae up," Cal said with a frown. "I have CIs on the ground whose jobs are to watch Medford's organization and report anything new or interesting."

Hal nodded. "Quick Kim and Fuzzy Phil."

Felly and I giggled. "Quick and fuzzy confidential informants?" I said. "I'd definitely pay for their info."

Hal gave me a look. "Those are aliases, Joey. They'd be in danger if Medford or any of his thugs ever found out they were squealing to us."

My smile died. "Got it." Still, Felly and I shared a look, and we laughed again.

"Who named them that?" Felly asked, lifting a brow at Cal.

His fine lips twitched again. "The aliases just came to mind, since they were quick and..."

"Fuzzy?" I asked, giggling again.

"Actually, yes," Hal agreed, finally sharing my smile. "Phil *is* pretty fuzzy."

"Anyway," Cal said, lowering his brows at Felly and me. "Phil has been reporting a lot of activity at Medford Industries. Lots of foreign power brokers going in and out. He thinks something's brewing."

"Big Daddy's away, so the children will play," Felly said.

"It's the new Animal House," I offered.

"I'm picturing Saudi Princes in togas," Felly said, waggling her brows.

"French diplomats in drag," I added.

We giggled again.

Cal and Hal shared a look.

"It might have been a mistake getting them together," Cal told his brother.

Hal eyed me, a suspicious glint in his pretty green eyes. "Yeah. I'm thinking it might be best if you stayed with me in the cabin and let these two goofs stay together at Joey's."

"Alone time! we said in unison, drawing dismayed looks from the Amitys.

To put the proverbial icing on the cake, Max chose that moment to set four plates of banana cream pie in front of us.

---

H al and Cal left us on my front porch after extracting multiple promises that we'd lock ourselves inside and call if we heard or saw anything at all. They changed their minds three times before we actually kicked them out and they finally left, their gazes sliding back to us one last time before the two men climbed into their respective cars and formed a short procession down my drive.

"I thought they'd never leave," Felly said with a

grin. Her breath left her mouth in frosty clouds, and her nose was slightly red from the cold. She stomped her feet on the porch floor to shake the snow off.

I put the key into the lock and turned it, my pibl slamming herself against the door from the inside, whining pitifully. "She knows you're here," I told Felly with a grin. "Are you ready for this?"

She chuckled, her pretty blue eyes sparkling. "Wait." Felly assumed a Sumo position and said, "go."

I turned the key and shoved the door open.

Caphy barreled past me and sailed into the air, tongue already swiping the air in anticipation of licking my cousin.

Felly's eyes went wide. Her mouth opened in a surprised "O" as the Pitbull flew toward her, whimpering with excitement. Despite the low, wide center of gravity she'd assumed, Felly still stumbled backward when Caphy hit, slamming her head into the remnants of a summer plant that was still hanging from a nearby porch column because I'd been remiss in getting rid of it.

Felly landed on her butt with a dog in her lap.

The plant swung wildly above her head, pitching dirt over them both. A beat later, weakened by the cold and probably already cracked, the plastic pot broke against the column it was hanging from and dumped frozen black dirt onto Caphy and Felly.

"Ah!" my cousin said, spluttering and spitting

dirt. She rubbed her head where the frozen part had connected. "I'm not gonna lie, that hurt."

Caphy sneezed and jumped off my cousin's lap, bounding away to do her business in the front yard — a.k.a. play in the snow.

I stood wide-eyed with my lips pressed together and one hand covering my mouth. "Are you okay?"

Felly grunted. She shoved dirt off her head and leaned back against the square white pillar. Scraping a plant root off her lips, she started laughing. "Well, she got me good that time."

I let my laugh escape too. "She did. I'm so sorry."

A small red ball rolled onto the porch, and a tiny black and white form slipped through the front door behind it. Felly gasped when Ethel Squeaks approached, her big ears twitching. "Hello, Ethel. Do you remember me?"

Felly and Ethel had met once, a few months after we'd adopted the little pig when her owner had been killed. Ethel had been a bit standoffish with everyone except Hal and me at the time. But after snuffling the pile of dirt next to Felly, her little tail started to twirl with happy greeting. She bounced over to her little ball and nosed it toward my cousin.

Felly looked at me.

"Yeah. It's what it looks like. She wants you to throw the ball for her."

"Hilarious. She's been around Caphy too long."

I shrugged. The pig had already been ball

obsessed when she came to us. But being around my goofy dog had definitely made her love the balls even more.

Felly threw the ball back into the house, and the pig scooted after it with a happy squeal.

A beat later, she was back.

"I probably should have warned you that you'll be her permanent ball slave now."

Felly snorted. "Story of my life." She threw it again and climbed painfully to her feet. "Has that dog gained some weight?"

I winced. "It's possible." More than possible, actually, since she regularly used her "poor pitiful pibl" look to beg, borrow, and steal more snacks than one dog should have.

Caphy bounded back just as LaLee sauntered onto the porch, her pink, feline nose firmly stuck into the air. The opinionated Siamese took one look at a dirt-coated Felly and snapped her tail as if to say, "don't come near me with your unfastidious self, hooman."

"Hello, Princess," Felly said. "I see you still have a stick of catnip up your posterior region."

"She does," I agreed. "Come on. I'll let you shower first. Then I have something I want to talk to you about." I grabbed her pretty rolling suitcase and tugged it into the house behind me.

"Yeah?" Felly asked, shaking like a dog to remove as much of the dirt as she could. "What's it about?"

"Come on, LaLee," I told the cat. Ignoring me as only a cat can, she walked away and rubbed herself along the Adirondack chair nearest the door. I sighed. I'd get Felly settled in her room and come back to corral the cat.

Chances were she'd already be inside the house. LaLee didn't really like being outside. She only pretended she did to annoy me.

I wished it didn't work so well. The cat was definitely cagier than I was.

When we came inside, Caphy was in play position, with her butt in the air. Ethel faced her with the ball under her snout, tail twirling.

"Your old room is ready," I told my cousin. "Does that work?"

"Perfect," she said, grinning.

Felly had spent many a summer at our house when we were growing up. She and I and my best friend Lis had enjoyed many a sunny summer day playing in the pond and woods together. On rainy days we'd built blanket forts, done each other's hair and makeup, and defeated a platoon of monsters in the dark, scary basement.

The thought brought back warm, wonderful memories.

"While you get cleaned up, I'll get stuff out to make chocolate chip cookies."

"And popcorn?" she asked, her eyes alight.

"And popcorn," I agreed happily. "We'll find a movie to stream."

She headed up the stairs to her room, and I started collecting stuff for cookies. It occurred to me that I should go clean up the dirt on the porch before LaLee walked through it and carried it inside.

Though fastidious to a fault, the cat wasn't averse to getting her paws messy if she could tweak me with the messy results. I grabbed a broom from the mud room and started toward the front. My cell rang. It was Hal.

"Hey, handsome. Are you having fun yet?"

"Tons. We're doing facials right now, then we're going to do our toenails and watch Love Actually. I'm all atwitter."

I grinned. "We're making cookies."

Silence beat through the line. "Chocolate chip cookies?"

"Yep. And popcorn."

"I'll send a minion over to fetch some."

"Uh, uh. This is a girls-only party. Make your own cookies."

"Joey, honey, it's a well-established fact that men are incapable of baking things. Our strength lies in eating already baked goods and in flattering the baker into repeating the baking process as often as humanly possible."

I snorted out a laugh. "Tell that to all the famous chefs in the world."

"Those men have given up their man cards to bake because they have to. I don't fault them. They're just playing to the market. But Cal and I are PIs. Our man cards are gilded and hanging in fire and bombproof frames on the wall. We can't be expected to bake."

"Uh-huh. But you're fine with eating said baked goods?"

"The man card has a long history on the acceptability of consuming baked goods. You know this."

I gave up trying not to laugh at him. "I'll tell you what. If you're very good, maybe Felly and I will bring you over a care package later."

"Good. You can bring my pig too. I forgot to grab her."

I sighed. "You drive a hard bargain, but..."

"Are you okay?" The sudden change in his tone made my belly tighten.

"I'm fine. Why?"

"I don't know. You just seemed...thoughtful earlier. Are you worried about Medford?"

"I'm not." It wasn't a lie. I wasn't worried about Garland Medford. I had no idea how I felt about the man, but he'd had lots of opportunities to hurt me, and he hadn't. Though the idea of his being around my mom was a bit terrifying. "I just hope my mom calls again so I can tell her not to come."

"Yeah. About that. I hope you don't mind. I told Arno what was going on, and asked him to see what he can find out about her. He was going to call Dev and grill him for info."

"Thanks for that. Dev might tell him more than he was willing to tell me." I had a feeling Devon Little was dealing with some rejection issues. I'd recently started to suspect that Dev had been in love with my mom for decades. He'd protected her ever since my dad died, even keeping her away from me until recently. He'd said it was to protect me, but I wasn't so sure about that. I suspected a part of him didn't want her around me because I was a reminder of her previous life and marriage. It still wasn't clear whether she returned his feelings. I was guessing her sudden disappearance was a vote in the *No* column on that. At least in his mind.

"I wanted to let you know that Cal touched base with his CI in Indy, and there's been no movement in the mansion. Nobody seems to be heading this way. If that changes, we'll know long before they arrive here. You can rest easy tonight and enjoy your sidekick."

"That's awesome."

"Yeah, it is. Also, Arno called me back on the coffee house guy..."

"Oh, what did he find out?"

"The guy fessed up after Arno leaned on him. He said a guy he'd never seen before offered him fifty dollars to pretend to bump into me and make a stink about it. He described the guy as around thirty, five eleven-ish, kind of wiry with wavy, reddish-brown hair. That's all he could give Arno. Does that sound like anybody you know?"

"No." The description reminded me of someone, but I couldn't put a finger on who.

"Okay, well, we'll keep our eyes open for the guy. Have fun with your cousin."

"I will. Thanks for checking into that for me."

"You're welcome, honey. See you and those cookies later?"

I laughed. "Only if you can make me believe that you're just as excited to see me as the cookies."

"Hey, I said you first."

"All clean," Felly said behind me. I turned to find her still toweling her damp hair.

"I have to go, Hal. Enjoy those pedicures. What color are you doing yours?"

"I thought I'd go with green to bring out the color of my eyes."

I laughed. "Sounds like a plan. Love you."

"I love you too," he said, a laugh in his voice. "See you later."

## 4

"I'm pretty sure I'm going to puke," Felly said.

I glanced over at her and winced. "You do look a little bit like Kermit the Frog."

Felly slapped my arm. "I'm going to assume you mean my color and not my bugged eyes and over-large mouth."

I shrugged. "You can do that. But remember what they say about assuming."

Felly chuckled and then groaned, holding her stomach. "Seriously though, do you have an antacid?"

I patted her knee and climbed to my feet. "Be right back."

I left her staring at a really bad horror movie on TV, the flickering lights of the movie playing over her face and exacerbating her Wicked Witch of the West hue. As I watched, she jammed a piece of popcorn between her lips. Stomach ache be darned. I grinned. It was fun having her there again.

Caphy was sprawled over Felly's lap on the couch, dead to the world. She didn't so much as flick an eyelid when I got off the couch.

Fickle creature.

LaLee was draped along the back of the couch. Her whipping tail had been smacking a lively cha, cha, cha on my cheek when I'd been seated—no doubt to keep me apprised of the fact that she didn't like strangers in her house.

Complaint noted and ignored. LaLee didn't like a lot of things.

The cabinet in the downstairs bathroom was empty of antacids. I made a mental note to stock up and trotted upstairs to my room.

I found the antacids in my bathroom and decided to take care of business while I was there. Popcorn always made me thirsty. And the two glasses of milk I'd had with the cookies added to the burden on my bladder.

I washed my hands and headed toward the door.

As I passed the bedroom window, light flared across the glass. Headlights on the road. I knew it wasn't Hal. He'd returned a couple hours earlier to get Ethel and as many cookies as Felly and I would let him steal. He apparently hadn't trusted me to bring them over.

Smart man.

I had to admit I was glad he'd come. If those cookies had stayed under my roof, I'd have eaten them. Then I'd be the same color as Felly.

I started for the door, jolting to a stop when light flashed over the window again. I redirected my steps to the window, climbing up on the padded window seat where I'd spent many a rainy day with Caphy, reading and watching the rain.

My pulse picked up when I spotted two arcs of light dancing over my yard. The light skimmed my Jeep, which was parked in the circular drive in front of the house, and caught the gleam of another vehicle parked on the other side of my car before continuing on toward the side of the house.

I glanced at the clock next to my bed. Midnight. A little late for visitors.

Unless they were up to no good.

I patted my pocket for my cell phone and grimaced.

I'd left it downstairs.

The two lights had split, one going around the south side of the house and one heading around the north side.

I ran for the stairs and jogged down, hitting the tile in front of the door and sliding to a stop as I reached to check the deadbolt. It was locked.

"What's going on?" Felly asked.

I jumped and spun, my heart trying to leap out of my throat. "You startled me."

She frowned. "What's going on, Joe?"

I pointed toward the kitchen. "Go. Check the lock on the kitchen door. I'm going to check the back."

As I started to jog down the hallway to the back door, the lights in the house went out. Silence pulsed as the television died.

The only sound coming from the living room was Caphy jumping down from the couch. Her claws danced a happy tune over the tile as she joined Felly and me. She was wagging her tail high and fast, and a low rumble played in her throat.

The front door shifted slightly in its frame and I stilled.

That had been a pressure change in the house. Someone had opened the back door.

I grabbed Felly's hand.

"They're inside," I told her. She gulped audibly. Caphy's growl deepened. I grabbed her collar and tugged her toward the kitchen door. "Come on," I whispered. My plan was to go out the kitchen door, which opened to the front of the house. My car keys were hanging from hooks in the mudroom. We'd get out of the house and drive the two miles to Hal's cabin.

It was a good plan. Except for the man who was standing in my kitchen when we hurried toward the mud room.

We skidded to a stop. Caphy snarled, lunging

toward the tall man whose features were obscured by the nearly complete darkness. Only the moonlight glancing off the snow in the yard allowed me to see the man at all. "Hush!" I told my dog. She only half-listened, allowing me to hold her back but still snarling.

Felly pressed close enough for me to feel the way she was vibrating. "Who are you?" Her voice shook, but I felt her reaching behind me toward the knife block on the counter.

I almost smiled. Armed with slavering Pitbull and a large knife. I liked our chances against one man.

The door in the mud room opened, pulling the clean scent of snow and a ribbon of moonlight into the room. But the man who stepped into the kitchen was in the shadows from the knees up. "We need to go, sir."

"I'll be there in a minute."

I knew that voice. Didn't I? "What are you doing here, Garland?" I asked.

Did I imagine the slight twitch of his shoulders when I used his name? Was he surprised I'd recognized his voice?

He lowered his head slightly, stepping closer but not close enough for Caphy's teeth to reach him. "Where's your mother, Joey?"

"What? Why? Are you threatening her?"

The door opened again. "Sir!"

The shadowed stranger in my kitchen seemed torn for a moment, unwilling to walk away.

Silence filled with deadly intent throbbed between us. Finally, I heard him sigh and he turned. "*I'm* not the one threatening her."

And then he was gone.

I ran after him and slammed the door closed, locking it. I ran past Felly as Caphy threw herself at the locked door, scratching and barking with canine frustration.

"What was that about?" Felly asked. She was scurrying along behind me as we made our way back to the living room by the light of the moon.

As I reached the couch where I'd left my phone, headlights painted the front window and washed away.

Felly ran to the window. "They're leaving."

Her words caused something to snap in my mind. Instead of calling Hal as I'd planned, I shoved the cell into the pocket of my jeans and ran toward the kitchen. "Come on!" I grabbed my coat and Felly's off the mudroom hooks, flinging Felly's to her.

"Where are we going?" Felly asked. To her credit, she didn't hesitate to follow me out of the house.

"We're going to follow them."

Caphy shot past me and started running up the drive. "Caphy, come!" She listened but only because

I opened the car door. To the pibl, riding in the car was almost more fun than biting a bad guy.

"Do you think that's a good idea?"

From the tone of Felly's voice, I could tell she didn't think so.

I let Caphy into the back seat. "Probably not," I admitted as I climbed into the driver's seat, shivering violently as the cold leather wrapped me in its frigid embrace. "But he mentioned my mom. He knows she's coming. That can't be good."

I started the Jeep and shot off down the drive, kicking up frozen gravel and skidding. I forced myself to slow down, or we'd end up with our tires buried in snow and mud at the side of the drive. As soon as I hit Goat's Hollow Road, I gunned it, following the too-distant glow of the intruders' tail lights.

"They're probably armed and we're not. Unless you count Caphy."

I did count Caphy in a pinch. But I was also resistant to the idea of her getting hurt. I'd almost lost my mind the one time before when she'd gotten shot trying to save me. I wasn't going through that ever again if I could help it. "We won't approach them. I just want to see where they're staying. Then we'll call Hal and Cal and Arno." I frowned. I didn't know if Arno could make anything stick. The men had broken into my house. Unless I'd forgotten to lock the door. It was possible I'd forgotten when I'd let Caphy out for her last potty break.

Maybe Arno could prove they'd cut the power to my house. Though the power sometimes died when it got too cold.

I sighed.

A smart man, and if I was dealing with Garland Medford, he was a very smart man, could easily talk his way out of charges. "I just want to ask him what he meant about my mom."

"I thought she was hiding somewhere," Felly said.

I nodded. "She was. Hopefully still is. But she called me. She said she'd be here soon. And then Dev called to tell me he was afraid she was heading this way."

"Oh no!" Felly said. "We need to stop her."

I spotted the car heading into Deer Hollow and hit the gas, trying to close the distance between us. The back tires skated across a patch of ice, and I fought to keep the car on the road.

Felly's hands slapped out, and she braced herself on the door and dashboard. "Whoa, girl. You might want to keep it below a hundred miles an hour. The road's getting slick."

"Sorry." I let up on the gas again. We were entering the city limits and the main drag through Deer Hollow was only thirty MPH.

I kept several car lengths between me and the

big car in front of us. Snow had begun to fall, obscuring my vision and making the road even slicker than before. Both hands white-knuckled on the steering wheel, I hoped the car wasn't heading back to Indy.

We passed the Brats versus Broads daycare building and kept going. One of the street lights was out, the victim of an almost continual onslaught by drunk high school boys who thought the lights made great targets for shooting practice.

We passed Sonny's Diner. The lights were off and snow blanketed the sidewalk outside the darkened building.

Louise Barker of Barkers Books was just coming out of her store as we passed by. She liked to do her paperwork at night after the store closed. Louise lifted her gaze and waved when she recognized my car.

As we passed out of Deer Hollow, the snow thickened to the point that I was struggling to see the road ahead. I hoped the thugs I was following didn't decide to stop quickly, or I might ram them before I knew they were there.

By the time we'd passed the gas station outside of town, I realized I could no longer see the taillights of the car I'd been following.

As we approached the new subdivision outside of town, the highway opened up in front of us, and I had to admit I'd lost them.

I slammed my palm down on the steering wheel. "Dangit!"

Felly reached over and squeezed my knee. "We'll figure this out, Joe. It's probably best that we don't confront these guys anyway. We're not exactly equipped for it."

I knew she was right. But I was still cranky about it.

I pulled into the subdivision and used one of the driveways to turn around. Backing onto the snow-covered street, I put the Jeep in drive and started off.

A black Suburban pulled out of a cross street and cut us off.

I threw on the brakes with a surprised yelp, skidding nearly to the SUV across the road before the Jeep stopped. Caphy slammed into the back of my seat and immediately righted herself, too worried about the car in front of us to even lament the fact that I'd made her face-plant.

Doors opened on both sides of the Suburban, and three men climbed out.

Felly grabbed her purse. "Joe?" Her voice quivered with nerves, but I noticed she shoved her hand into her purse.

"What have you got in there?" I asked.

"I have mace. I'd rather not get that close to them though, unless it's necessary."

I wiggled my fingers at her. "I'll take it."

Her startled gaze met mine, blue eyes shot wide. "Are you sure?"

"Yes."

She felt inside the purse and came up with the canister, handing it to me.

Then she reached back inside and pulled out a knife in a sheath. "What are you, Killer Mary Poppins?" I squeaked. "What else do you have in there?"

She winced. "I could have brought my gun but Cal talked me out of it. Dang him."

I jumped at a loud tap on my window.

A man's hand, wearing a large metal ring, tapped again.

Caphy snarled, flinging herself at the window of the back seat and barking in agitation.

"Don't open it!" Felly said, brandishing her knife to the man who'd come up alongside the Jeep on her side.

He chuckled darkly and then dropped from sight. Felly leaned closer to the window. "Where'd he go?"

The car wobbled, and the man reappeared. He walked around the back of the Jeep. Caphy flung herself against the seat, half snarling and half barking but not sure which man to focus on.

The man at my window tapped his big ring against the glass again.

I put it down an inch, holding the mace up between us. "What do you want?"

He wore a black ski mask, which made it impossible to identify him. But his voice still seemed familiar. Though I'd decided it wasn't Garland Medford after all. He was too slender and moved like a younger man. "Why are you following us?"

My hand felt like ice around the canister. I really wished it was a gun instead. With all the bad stuff that had happened to me lately, Hal had insisted on giving me shooting lessons out behind his cabin. I was glad he had. Shooting a gun made me feel less helpless. "I wasn't following you."

The man cocked his head. The lips I could see through the mouth hole quirked into a smile. "You just had a hankerin' to go for a drive on a night not fit for man nor beast?"

Unable to come up with a good excuse, I instead took the offensive to distract him. "What's with the mask? Don't you think that's a little overly-dramatic?"

He patted the knit mask and chuckled. "It's very warm. You have cold winters here in Deer Hollow, Indiana."

I caught the tinge of an accent when he said *Indiana.* "I guess you come from warmer climes?" I raised my chin, trying to look unafraid. Though the hand holding the mace was shaking violently.

Caphy continued to assault the inside of my car,

spraying spittle over my windows as the men moved freely around the Jeep.

The car wobbled a couple more times, and then the two men who'd climbed out with Mr. Mask gave him a nod and returned to their car. One of them slid something long and dark into his coat pocket before climbing inside.

Mr. Mask tapped the glass one more time. "Heed my warning about your mom, Joey. And don't try to find us again. It won't go well for you."

He turned and walked away, his stride filled with cocky assurance that made me want to scream.

I waited until they were heading out of the subdivision before I put the car into drive and started after them.

"Have you lost your mind?" Felly asked, the knife still clutched in her white-knuckled hand.

The car bumped awkwardly forward, making a weird chugging-flapping noise as I tried to accelerate.

"Dangit!" It didn't take me long to realize what the men had done. I climbed out of the car and eyed the four flat tires of my car. Slamming my palm on the roof, I made Caphy bark again.

Felly got out and sighed. "They sliced your tires. Jerks!"

"Yeah," I agreed, pulling the phone out of my pocket. "That's one name for them." I could think of a few others. I dialed Hal, knowing the call wasn't going to be a fun one. He was going to be very unhappy with me for taking off without him.

"Hey, honey," he said, sounding tired. "Did you miss me?"

I closed my eyes, pulled in a bracing breath, and climbed back into the car. "Hey, sorry to interrupt your facials..."

## 5

Hal dropped Caphy and me off at my house two hours later. We'd had to wait almost an hour for the tow truck from the Greasy Wrench to come and get my car. There had apparently been two crashes on the highway from the ice building up on the roads.

Most of that time, Hal had spent grilling me about the men who'd broken into my house and slashed my tires. He hadn't been happy about my responses. I didn't know much more than the model and color of their car. I hadn't even been able to see the license plate in the heavy snow.

I did share my suspicion that the man in the mask had a slight accent and that he'd reminded me of Garland Medford.

"You're probably just projecting about the Medford thing," he'd said, frowning.

"What does that mean?" I'd objected, taking offense.

He held up a hand. "I didn't mean anything insulting, honey. I'm just saying that Medford's on your mind and then this happens. It's human nature."

I shook my head, irritated but not able to disagree. I knew that made sense. But I also knew that wasn't it. The man did remind me of Garland. Maybe they were distantly related or something. "I wish he'd taken off that stupid mask even for a minute."

Hal parked in my snow-covered turnaround and opened his door. "If he had, you probably wouldn't be alive to talk about it."

There was that.

I looked at him. "Did Cal bring Felly back here?"

Hal's gaze slid from mine. He climbed out and came around the car, letting me out and waiting while Caphy jumped out and ran into the yard, playfully bounding around in the snow before settling down to do her business.

"Hal?" I asked, nudging him for a response.

"He took her to the cabin."

I frowned. "She's staying with me."

"Honey..."

I turned around and stomped toward the house. "I'm going to call her and make him bring her back."

Hal caught up with me. "You two make bad decisions together."

I fixed a glare on him that had him scrubbing a hand over his face. I ignored the weariness in his handsome face because I wanted to be mad. There was no room for pity at the moment. "Don't treat me like a child." My voice was soft, throbbing with anger.

"Then don't act like one." His expression showed regret as soon as the words came out.

I narrowed my gaze on him for a moment and then spun on my heel, heading up the steps with my head throbbing from a rush of angry blood and my hands fisted.

"Joey…" he called out, but I didn't want to talk to him.

I unlocked the front door and stepped inside. I'd kicked off my boots and tugged off my coat before I realized I wasn't alone in the entry.

My head jerked toward the slight figure standing half in shadow. I gave a yelp of surprise.

The figure stirred and stepped forward, the golden illumination of the chandelier above our heads gilding her as she gave me an apologetic smile. "I'm sorry to startle you, sweetie."

"Mom!" I dropped the coat I'd been removing onto the floor and ran to her, wrapping her into my arms and hugging her tight. She felt like she'd lost weight, but she smelled as she always had, of violets and the fresh outdoors. Her hair, a silky strawberry blonde like mine, showed no sign of the gray strands I'd noticed the last time we'd been together. It was freshly colored and styled in a long, smooth bob that flattered her slender face. Taller than me by three inches, my mom had always been slender and pretty in a down-to-earth way.

But the woman standing in front of me looked more elegant than earthy, with a well-cut cream pantsuit over a vee-necked silk shirt in the palest peach. Her narrow feet were covered in silk pumps that matched the shirt and her slender hands were soft, the nails perfectly manicured.

"You look different," I told her.

She stepped away from me, keeping hold of my hands. "You look exactly the same." She gave me a gentle smile. "As beautiful as always."

The front door opened and my mother's eyes went wide. She stepped quickly back, blending into the shadows of the hall.

"It's okay, mom. It's just Hal."

Nails clattered on the tile and Caphy barreled toward us, tongue lolling and tail whipping in delight. I managed to grab the pibl's collar and drag her to a stop before she launched herself at my mom.

"Did you say mom?" Hal asked, his green gaze searching the shadows behind me. The hallway leading to the kitchen and a small half-bath, as well as the back door, was unlit.

I nodded. "It's safe. You can come out."

My mother slowly reemerged, giving Hal a nod. "Mr. Amity."

I frowned at the formality. My mother and Hal had gotten along famously when she and Dev had shown up to surprise me at Christmas time. In fact, Hal had been the one to invite them as a Christmas present to me.

"Joline," he said, smiling. "You look amazing."

The ice melted from my mother's expression. She gave a girlish laugh, moving forward to give Hal a hug. "There's no point telling you the same. You'll just get a big head. I'm sure you already know that you're devastatingly handsome."

Tears burned my eyes.

Hal bowed his head, embarrassed. "Devastatingly is a little over the top. But coming from you, I'm honored. How have you been?"

"Good." She nodded as if to give weight to the answer. But I saw the tightness in her jaw, the stiff way she held herself.

"Dev called," I told her. "He's worried."

Her smile slid away. I was sorry for it. But Devon had saved her life on several occasions. He deserved better.

"I'll call him."

"Good." I looped my arm through hers. "Would

you like coffee?"

"Maybe some wine?"

I laughed. "Even better." I looked at Hal. He was watching me to see if I was still mad.

I don't think my mom could miss the tension between us. She touched my arm. "If you don't mind, I'd like to use the ladies' room first?"

"Of course. You know where it is?" We shared a grin. The house had belonged to her and my dad long before I'd inherited it. "I'll be in the kitchen."

As she disappeared down the hallway, I turned to Hal. "I'm sorry."

He frowned. "Me too. I handled that badly. I promise I wasn't trying to bully you. Felly was tired, and I didn't know how long we'd be. Cal suggested he take her home just for tonight. They'll be back for breakfast in the morning."

"Just them?" I asked, worried he was angry and wouldn't come with them.

He grinned widely. "I'll already be here, sleeping on your couch. If you don't mind. I was going to anyway. But with your mom here..."

I nodded, feeling instantly better. "That would make me feel a lot better." I lifted onto my tippy toes and gave him a lingering kiss. "Thank you."

"Any time, beautiful. Now," he wrapped an arm around my waist. "How about that wine?"

Saying he had some work to do, Hal had gone into the living room with his laptop.

Mom and I sat on the tall stools at my kitchen island, sipping the last of our wine. Between the three of us, we'd polished off an entire bottle of Cabernet Sauvignon, and I was feeling warm and drowsy. But I needed to talk to my mom about what she was up to, and since she'd had most of that bottle herself, I figured she was lubed up enough to spill.

"Why did you come to Deer Hollow, mom?" I asked into the comfortable silence between us.

She blinked, looking surprised. "What are you talking about, sweetie? I came to see you."

I smiled, clasping her hand and giving it a squeeze. "That's so nice." I lowered my brows. "Such a nice lie."

Mom choked on her wine and succumbed to a bout of coughing. I pounded her on the back for a minute and then got up to pour a glass of water. Giving her the glass, I crossed my arms and waited.

As soon as she could breathe again, my mom laughed, shaking her head. "It's like I'm talking to your father." The smile faded. I assumed because her words had brought his memory into sharp focus for a moment. She cleared her throat and sighed. "Dev was suffocating me. I just needed to get away for a while."

I watched her twirl the glass between her fingertips for a minute. "Is that the truth?"

Her gaze jerked up to mine. Anger, uncertainty, worry, and an array of other emotions cycled through her blue gaze. I waited for her to settle on one.

When I didn't relent, my mom sighed. "It's definitely part of the truth."

"Then tell me the rest. You're in danger here, Mom. As happy as I am to see you, coming here was a mistake."

Tears glistened in her eyes. "It seems I'm not safe anywhere anymore."

"What does that mean?"

She shook her head, scraping the tears off her cheeks with the heel of her hand and sniffling. "Nothing. I'm just tired. I'm feeling sorry for myself."

"Tell me, mom. I can't help you if you won't tell me."

She shook her head. "I'm going to bed. Where do you want me?"

I felt guilty making her sleep in a guest bedroom when I was sleeping in her old room. "You can have your room. But you might have a visitor in the middle of the night."

Her eyes went wide, and she glanced toward the door, clearly mistaking my meaning.

I laughed. "Not Hal. I was talking about LaLee.

Just a word of warning, don't try to move her when she takes over the whole bed. She'll bite you."

My mother glowered at the feline, who was draped over the wide sill of the bowed window overlooking the back yard. The soft light of the recessed lighting over the sink reflected against the glass, obscuring any ability to see into the dark yard beyond, but the cat had been staring out there anyway, tail whipping against the wall beneath the sill as if she could see perfectly well.

Mom shook her head. "That's your room now, sweetie. I'll sleep in your old room if that's okay?"

I nodded. "There are fresh towels and things in the bathroom." Then I had a thought. "Do you have a bag?"

She nodded. "I left it in the back hall."

"How'd you get here? There's no car out front."

Her gaze skimming quickly away, she flipped a dismissive hand. "I caught an Uber. I'll see you in the morning, Joey."

"Night, mom."

I watched her go, feeling all kinds of dissatisfied by our little chat. It was as clear as day that she wasn't telling me everything. She might even be outright lying to me. It wasn't like her to lie to me. I didn't think. Then, with a frustrated sigh, I realized she'd probably been lying to me all my life.

I was just getting too cynical to believe the lies anymore.

---

## 6

Felly and Cal showed up at my house at nine in the morning. I'd set up five places around my dining room table since we had too many for my small table in the kitchen to hold. Hal was cooking because I'd learned during our time together that he was a better cook than I was. But that wasn't saying much. To give him his due, he was an excellent cook.

He'd made two quiches, one ham and swiss cheese and the other veggie, which was bursting with onions, sweet red peppers, and fat chunks of portobello mushrooms with feta cheese. The kitchen smelled delicious.

Felly had called to say they'd bring homemade cinnamon rolls and fruit salad.

When I returned to the kitchen, Hal was sliding thin-sliced potatoes with the skins on into my biggest frying pan. The pan already sizzled with glossy caramelized onions.

"That smells delicious," I told him, wrapping my arms around his waist and resting my head against his warm back. "Especially since I don't have to cook."

He grabbed one of my hands and kissed the palm. "You're in charge of juice and coffee." He ground fresh pepper and pink sea salt over the potatoes. "Do you think we need toast?"

"Maybe a few slices. Felly's bringing cinnamon rolls, but I'm not sure my mom will eat sweets for breakfast."

Hal gave me an exaggerated look of horror. "You must be adopted."

"Har de har har," I told him, a smile twitching on my lips. "Besides, you should be happy for my sweet tooth. Sweets make me sweet."

He kissed my palm again. "Now back off. I'm afraid this oil will spatter your hands and burn you."

I tugged on the frilly apron I'd bought him that said, "Kiss the cook," and stepped away. "At least you're wearing protection."

"I've been around the block a few times."

Caphy jumped up from her favorite spot under the kitchen table and barked once, her tail wagging with excitement.

"Who's here, girl?" I asked in a high-pitched play voice.

She bounced, whining once and then dancing halfway to the door before running back to try to entice me to come with.

"Let them in, beauty," Hal told her, grinning as she took off like a shot to the door.

Much nail clacking, furry chest smacking, and helpless giggling later, Cal called out. "We're here!"

"In the kitchen," his brother responded.

I'd fully expected Hal to take his apron off before his brother saw him, but he didn't. I thought the fact that he was so unselfconscious was adorable.

The first one through the kitchen door was Ethel Squeaks. She trotted toward me with a smile on her tiny black and white face, ears twitching and tail spinning like a top. She looked five pounds heavier but plenty warm in her black and red buffalo check sweater with the turtle neck.

"Good morning, pretty girl," I told her, dropping to my knees to let her push against me in her version of a hug.

Felly followed, carrying a pan covered in foil. The enticing scent of cinnamon, butter, and yeast followed her into the room.

Caphy was glued to her leg, nearly tripping her as she tried to walk. "This dog is just about diving into the pan," she complained with a smile.

I took it from her, setting it on the stove so the heat from the other burner could keep the rolls warm. "She's really just happy to see *you*," I told my cousin.

"Uh-huh." Felly looked around. "Where's your mom?"

I'd called Felly the night before, happy she was still awake so we could discuss the night's events and speculate together over them. Felly's take on my mom's situation was that she either didn't trust Dev anymore, or she believed trouble was getting too close and she thought leaving would keep him safe. That theory didn't make me feel any better. By that train of thought, she was willingly putting me in danger instead.

By the time I'd hung up, I'd had trouble getting to sleep. My mind was swirling with intrigue and worry.

"She hasn't come down yet. She looked pretty tired last night."

Felly lowered her voice and leaned close. "Do you think she called Devon?"

Cal came into the kitchen, his face red from the cold. "Did you guys know you have a crop circle in your front yard?"

We all just stared at him until he grinned. "No, really. It's a big circle where all the snow is blown away. If I had to guess, a chopper landed out there last night."

I t was times like this when I wished I had closer neighbors who were nosy like Gladys Kravitz from Bewitched. It would have been really hard for anybody to miss a helicopter landing in my yard.

Especially me.

I looked at Hal. "Felly and I were here. We would have heard a chopper land."

"Except for when you took off after those guys," he reminded me.

"True." I frowned, "But that doesn't explain who would land a chopper in my yard and why."

"There's no chance the guys who broke into your house came here in a chopper?" Cal asked.

Felly and I both gave him a look.

He raised his hands. "I come in peace."

Felly snorted. "No way. We'd have heard something. Seen the lights."

"Caphy would have had kittens," I told him, shaking my head. "No, Hal's right. This had to be during that three-hour window while we were gone."

"Which is a very lucky coincidence for somebody," Hal said. His gaze swung to his brother's. "Or a very detailed plan."

I thought about that. "You think those guys who broke into my house were a distraction?"

Hall shrugged. "Anybody who knows you would know that you'd probably follow them."

"But what if I hadn't?" I said.

"Then they'd have tried something else," Cal said. "The real question is why? Is there anything missing in the house?"

"I don't know. I didn't check. I just assumed those guys broke in to give me a warning about mom."

"Okay, let's start there," Hal said. "We'll see if they took something. If not, then we have to assume the person in the chopper was here for other reasons."

I didn't have to ask what other reasons. I was afraid I already knew. They were looking for my mom.

That hadn't taken long.

My mother was sitting at the island drinking coffee when we came back inside. She looked up and smiled, her cell phone on the counter in front of her. A quick glance at the screen told me she'd been perusing her favorite online news sites. "Morning, sweetie."

I kissed her cheek. "Did you sleep okay?"

"Like the dead. I'd forgotten how quiet it is here."

*Yeah*, I thought. *Except when people are breaking in, or helicopters are landing in the yard.*

I rubbed her back. "Hungry? Hal cooked a wonderful breakfast."

The front door opened amid much laughter. My

dog clattered down the hall as if she'd already scented my mom. She bounded inside, tail whipping, and jumped up to put her paws on mom's lap.

"Oh!" Mom exclaimed. "Your paws are cold."

"Auntie Fulle!" Felly squealed from the kitchen door. Her cheeks were bright red and her streaked light-brown hair was crusted with ice. She hurried over and hugged my mom, a chunk of hard-pack snow falling from the icy nest on her head as she did.

"What happened to you?" I asked my cousin, laughing.

"Snowball fight," she said happily. "I won!"

Leaning against the doorframe, Cal arched a midnight brow. "Won is a relative term. Siccing the Pitbull on me and then shoving ice down my shirt while I'm fighting off a tongue up my nostrils doesn't count."

Felly's grin was unrepentant. "Says who!"

I slapped her five. "Let's eat," I said, sliding my friends a meaningful look. "Food's getting cold." My non-verbal message was that we'd eat breakfast first and then engage a search of the house. Then, I needed to get my mom alone and try to get her to talk honestly about what was going on.

But we'd eat first. I needed my strength to get me through what was likely to be an uncomfortable conversation.

F elly kept my mom distracted while Hal and I did a quick search of the house. All of my electronics were still where they should be. The little bit of jewelry I had that was worth anything, most of it inherited from my mom after her faux death, was still tucked into the toe of one of my dad's old tube socks and hidden beneath my yoga pants in a drawer. I left it out on top of my dresser so I'd remember to give it back to her.

All paintings and artwork that had any value were still in their assigned spots, though some of it I'd be happy to have stolen, particularly my mom's dozens of ceramic statues in the curio cabinet in the living room. The little painted figurines were still staring out at me from the glass-sided cabinet, with their pink pudgy cheeks and wide blue eyes.

Dust catchers all.

Hal came into the living room and shook his head to tell me that the silver in the dining room hutch was still intact.

That was it. Whatever those men had been doing in my house the night before, they hadn't come to steal from me. I hadn't really believed that was why they were there, but it had to be ruled out.

I turned to my mom, who was sitting on the couch with my cousin, giggling over the picture album of Felly, Lis, and me when we were growing up. I wished Lis weren't out of town at a realtor convention. She'd have loved to spend time with Felly.

I'd just have to make Felly come back again. Or Lis and I would go to Indianapolis to see Felly.

Girl's weekend!

"Mom," I said in as cheerful a voice as I could muster, "I need to take Caphy for a walk. Would you like to join us?"

Her expression brightened. "I'd love to. It would feel good to stretch my legs." She patted Felly's knee. "You should come too, honey."

Felly's gaze met mine. I gave her a little head shake. There was no way my mother would open up about her situation with Devon if Felicity was there.

Felly opened her mouth to respond, but Cal interrupted. "She'll have to join you on the next one," he said, giving my mother a devastating smile. "She promised to come to the grocery with me. We're in charge of the salad for tonight's dinner, and I don't know my romaines from my arugulas."

Mom laughed gaily. "You men. You're all such carnivores."

"Guilty as charged," Hal said. He kissed me on the temple. "I think I'll go with them. You don't mind walking Caphy without me?"

I gave him a grateful smile. "You go on. Don't let Felly get French dressing for the salad. She's got five-year-old tastebuds for salad dressing."

"Hey!" my cousin objected, her eyes alight. "I'll have you know I've graduated to Russian dressing. I'm all growed up."

Cal looked down his Greek nose at her shortness. "You're not all *that* growed up, Princess. I can still fit you into one of my pockets."

She slapped him on the stomach, and he made an exaggerated "Umph!" sound. "Just try it, Adonis. I'll put a kink in that perfect nose of yours."

As they headed toward the door, still arguing playfully, I turned to my mom. "You want to borrow boots and gloves and stuff?"

She nodded. "Thanks, sweetie. That would be great."

---

The air was crisp and clean. The sun was bright against the snow. Even with sunglasses, I found myself squinting underneath it. The woods looked like a winter wonderland, the naked branches painted in a thin veneer of sparkling frost. Deer tracks littered the snow around the path, keeping Caphy in a perpetual state of excitement that she was going to catch something big.

We laughed at her antics. She ran with her nose to the ground, snorting and sneezing as she sucked more snow than air.

Between all that snorting and her occasional cacophony of excited barks at the retreating squirrels, there was no way my pitty was going to sneak up on anything in that woods.

Mom slid her arm through mine and laid her head on my shoulder. "This is nice. Thanks for inviting me."

I gave her arm a squeeze. "I'm glad you came. I've missed you."

"I've missed you too, sweetie. So much." She lifted a bright smile to me. "In fact, I think I'm going to stay in Deer Hollow for a while."

Shock stalled my response. We walked on in a tense silence for several minutes before I managed to respond. "I'm not sure it's safe for you here, Mom."

She tugged her arm from mine and bent to pick up an ice-covered stick, yelling, "Caphy, girl!" She waited for the goofy canine to whip around and then threw the stick into the trees.

Caphy bounded happily after it, her muscular body easily cutting through the spots where the wind had blown the powdery snow into three-foot-high drifts.

We walked on, neither of us speaking.

I began to realize my mother wasn't going to speak first, so I took the initiative. "You can't just ignore the danger, Mom."

She turned an angry look on me. "What danger, Joey? I swear you sound just like Dev."

Judging by the tone of her voice, that wasn't a good thing.

"Well, if I do, it's because he's right. We still don't know who's after you."

She stiffened, her gloved hands clenching into angry fists. "Yes, Joey. We do know. And he's gone. I'm sick of hiding. I'm sick of letting a bunch of thugs determine how I live my life. I'm over it..." She stopped talking as tears slid from her blue eyes. "I'm not going to do it anymore."

I pulled her into a hug. "I'm sorry."

She sniffed, shaking her head, and pushed me gently away. "It's not your fault. I know you're trying to protect me. Don't you see, that's the problem. Everybody's protecting me. Everybody has altered their lives to keep me safe. I'm nothing but a weight around everybody's necks. I don't want to be Devon's problem anymore. I don't want to be your problem, sweetie." Her voice softened and she grabbed my hands, squeezing my fingers in accompaniment to the urgency of her words. "It's time I stood on my own and took back my life."

I took a deep breath, my own tears sliding down my cheeks and freezing there. "Is this why you and Devon fought?" I asked her. "He doesn't think you're safe?"

She turned away and started walking again, her posture stiff. "It doesn't matter what Devon thinks. It's my life. It only matters what I think."

I didn't want to break her newfound backbone. It seemed cruel. But if I didn't, she was going to get herself killed. I followed her, walking slowly as I struggled with what I needed to do.

Caphy blasted out of the trees with the stick in her mouth, her ears flopping as she bounded through the snow like it wasn't even there. She dropped the stick in front of my mom and bounced back, eyes bright and tongue lolling in happy expectation. Mom didn't disappoint. She picked it up and threw it again.

Before I knew what I was going to say, I was saying it. "They broke into my house last night, mom. They threatened me. They told me you were in danger."

My mom went very still. She turned slowly to face me. I expected to see fear on her face. I expected anger. Disappointment. But what I saw there was guilt.

So. Much. Guilt.

I sucked in a gasp, feeling my world spinning around my feet. I closed my eyes and then opened them again, forcing myself to look her in the eyes. "What have you done?" I asked her.

She couldn't meet my gaze, but tears glistened in her eyes.

"Tell me."

She shook her head, sniffled, and then finally started to talk. "I..."

An ominous *thwup, thwup, thwup* sound broke the icy stillness in the air. The trees around us swayed in an unnatural wind, the snow sifting from their branches like fairy dust.

My heart jumping into my throat, I jerked my gaze toward the sky.

A chopper drifted into view over the tops of the trees, and I could see a figure dressed all in black braced in the open door of the aircraft. The distinctive shape of a rifle protruded from his hands.

And he was aiming it in our direction.

## 7

"Caphy!" I screamed, my voice lost in the bass rumble of the lowering chopper.

The ground geysered up inches from my mom's feet, spraying us with a mix of dirt and ice.

Caphy emerged from the trees at a gallop, barking at the trouble she scented and heard on the air.

Another burst of dirt and snow geysered up, the second bullet slicing the air mere inches from my cheek.

I grabbed my mom's arm, realizing we were sitting ducks out in the open. "Run!"

It was slow going in the snow once we left the path. The wind had mounded it up around the trees. The morning sun had warmed it enough to create an icy crust that bit at our boots and scraped along our legs as we ran.

My dog was jumping into the air, snarling at the chopper and the man half hanging from its frame. I watched in horror as the gunman raised the rifle to sight it again, realizing he was sighting it on Caphy.

I gave mom a shove. "Into the trees!"

I didn't wait to see if she listened. Our only hope was to hide in the trees and hope the chopper gave up and left.

Barely slowing as I reached her, I bent down and snatched up Caphy's leash, which was stiff from the cold and covered in debris from dragging through the snow. "Come on, girl!" I screamed, my voice buried under the throb of the chopper blades.

The side of a large tree exploded as mom ran past. She gave a short scream of fear and stooped, ducking behind the wide trunk as I caught up, dragging Caphy in my wake.

My dog didn't want to run away. She wanted to fight the men invading her territory. I didn't blame her, but I'd learned the hard way not to bring teeth and claws to a gunfight.

The wind whipped the frosty bushes around us into a frenzy. I realized the chopper had landed in the small clearing where we'd been.

*Dangit!*

I grabbed my mom's arm. "We need to run."

"Where are we going to go, Joey?" she demanded, clearly scared and frustrated.

I shook my head, thinking fast, and realized the

only possible place was Hal's cabin. But it was two miles through the woods. And the terrain got pretty rough at times. We'd never make it.

Still, it was our only chance. "Come on," I started running, keeping as many trees between us and the gunman as possible. If we were lucky, he'd decide he didn't want to make his way through the woods on foot.

Then I had a thought. "Here, hold her a minute." I handed the leash to my mom and tugged out my cell. A quick glance told me I had no bars. We rounded a large boulder and I stopped, quickly typing a text to Hal. *Chopper, guns, running to the river. 4x4. Hurry!*

Hopefully, he'd be able to interpret my abbreviated message. There was no time to explain.

I looked at my mom. "I have an idea. It's not a fun idea, but it might save us."

"Whatever you think, sweetie," my mom said, panting and looking paler than she should. "You've always known these woods better than me."

I nodded and took Caphy's leash back. "River, Caphy."

She took off like a shot, tongue lolling in a sloppy doggy grin. I rarely let her go to the river because the undercurrents could be deadly, and the coyotes that formed their dens in the rocky ridge that framed it even deadlier.

But at that moment, the men with guns were

much deadlier than the possibility of running into a coyote.

We really had no choice.

Behind us, shouting told me the men had decided to pursue us on foot.

*Awesome sauce.*

The sound spurred us on, and I was grateful Caphy didn't bark at the voices.

We started hearing the growl of the river after only a few minutes. Fifteen minutes later, we burst out of the trees and I grabbed my mom's arm before she plunged into the icy water. I didn't remember it being so close to the trees. But we'd had a ton of rain over the previous week before the temps dropped and it had turned to snow. The river was bloated with the extra rain, and moving fast.

A thick, yellowish froth sat on top of the shallow water at the edges and painted the clusters of tree debris that had been ripped away by the rampaging water.

I could barely hear the throb of chopper blades above the roar of the river. They were searching for us by air too.

My heart sank.

I tugged my cell out to see if I had bars and saw a text from Hal. *Called Arno. Coming from my house with 4x4. Stay down and hidden.*

My chest loosened at the sight. I glanced at mom. "Hal's coming. He called Arno."

The tree closest to me exploded, firing bark and ice at us like a thousand tiny bullets. Pain etched its way over my neck and cheek, and mom fell with a cry of pain.

Caphy tried to jerk free. I barely managed to hold on. "No!" I told her. "Be still."

I reached down and grabbed my mom's arm. "Are you okay?"

She swiped a gloved hand over her throat and looked at the blood. "Yeah. It just surprised me."

I eyed the shallows where a wide creek met the raging river and chewed my lip. I'd hoped we could hunker down and wait for Hal and Arno. But there was no time. "We need to cross here."

"Cross?" Mom brushed snow from her jeans and stared at the fast-moving creek water. "Why?"

I pointed to the rocky cliff on the opposite side. It was pocked in a hundred spots by small indentations cut into the surface over the decades by driving water and natural erosion. The coyotes used them for dens. We were going to use one of them as a hidey-hole. "If we can get inside one of those before they spot us, we can hide until the cavalry gets here."

Mom nodded.

Just then, the chopper burst from the tree cover above our heads. I grabbed mom and threw her backward in the snow, yanking the leash to bring Caphy with us. We were under the tree cover but only just. If the men in the chopper looked very hard, they'd see us.

I rolled beneath the snowy branches of an evergreen, hoping my white coat would camouflage us in the snow. Caphy lay down next to us, panting and bright-eyed. I didn't think she'd stand out much with her blonde coat, but just in case, I pulled snow up around us.

Someone shouted in the woods, our pursuers communicating location as they searched. The fact that they didn't seem worried about us hearing them encased my spine in ice.

They were much too confident they'd find us.

The chopper moved slowly along the river, their blades forming smooth circles on the surface of the raging water.

We were caught in the middle of them, unable to move forward or back.

My heart pounded painfully against my ribs. A simple, heartfelt plea to Hal repeated itself inside my head. *Hurry, hurry, hurry...*

The rumble of an engine cut through the chopper's retreating noise, and my head came up.

"Is that Hal?" my mom whispered, hope in her voice.

"I don't know."

We jumped as a shot rang out.

The engine roared as it came closer. More gunfire peppered the woods. Men shouted.

Someone screamed in pain. The sound of running and heavy breathing made me push to my knees. Someone was coming closer, and I wasn't sure who it was.

"We need to move," I said, climbing to my feet.

A man burst through the trees, a rifle in his hands. He was limping as he ran, and his face was filled with fear.

When he spotted us, his expression changed. He smiled. The sight twisted terror into my gut.

I shoved my mom behind me and gave her the leash. "Go! Take Caphy."

"I'm not leaving you," she said, steel in her voice.

"Mom!"

"No." She stepped up beside me. "I'm not leaving you to deal with my mess. Not anymore."

The man lifted the rifle, sighted it, and a bullet exploded into the icy air.

"Ah!" I screamed, ducking and covering my ears.

The gun had gone off from somewhere behind us. Much too close. And my ears were ringing.

To my shock, the man with the rifle jerked and folded toward the ground.

Caphy erupted in snarls and barking, nearly tugging free of my grip.

Realizing too late what had happened, I swung around.

And came face to face with Garland Medford.

## 8

I shoved myself in front of mom, keeping Caphy's leash short.

Garland was standing near the water, the icy liquid splashing up to spot his jeans and heavy boots. He was holding a gun, and his eyes were locked on my mom.

"Hello, Joline."

Her mouth tightened, and she lifted a hand toward him as if imploring him not to shoot. Her action made him frown. He looked down at the gun, blinking. "Oh. Sorry." Medford shoved the gun into a holster beneath his heavy coat. "Come on, I have a four-wheeler. We need to get out of here before the chopper returns."

He held out a hand and, to my shock, my mom took it, letting him pull her in close and press a kiss to her forehead. "You scared me."

She sighed, relaxing against him. "I didn't think you'd get here in time."

Caphy and I watched them with our mouths open like we were watching a train wreck and couldn't look away. *What the...?*

Caphy whined and looked up at me. She gave one hesitant, confused swipe of her tail and then dropped to her butt in the snow.

I knew how she felt. Throwing up my hands, I said. "Hold on, here. What am I missing?"

Garland's well-sculpted lips curved upward. He gave me a look that felt like pity. It made me very uncomfortable. "I'm sorry, Joey. I know this must be confusing, but this isn't the time or place. We need to go."

"Go where?" I asked. Frustration made the words come out in a growl.

*Thwup, thwup, thwup.*

Garland's gaze lifted to the sky and he swore. "They're coming back. Joey, you're just going to have to trust me."

"I'm not trusting you."

Mom moved away from him and took my hands. "Then, will you trust me?"

Her gaze was lit with excitement. Her cheeks were pink, and her red-gold hair curled softly around her face. She looked twenty years younger than she had when she'd arrived on my doorstep. "Please, sweetie. I promise it's safe."

My brows peaked. "Safe?" Anger stalled the breath in my lungs and flooded my face with color. "*We know who was trying to kill me, Joey,*" I said, my voice throbbing with anger. "*He's gone. I want to live my life.*" I bit the words out, repeating what she'd said to me earlier. She'd lied right to my face. It stung.

My mother paled, guilt etched across her features.

"And you want me to trust you," I said.

She jerked her gaze toward the guy bleeding in the snow behind me. "You're right, sweetie. But can we talk about it later? You'll be safe with us. Safer than alone or with those people. I promise I'll explain everything. Just come. Okay?"

I shook my head, my jaw tight. "Hal and Arno are coming."

We moved closer to the trees, pressing into the icy branches as the helicopter glided toward us. The chopper followed the winding ribbon of water, heading back the way it had come.

"They're going to regroup," Garland told us. "It won't take them long to figure out they should follow the road. We need to get to my car."

"They who?" I asked, sounding frustrated even to my ears.

Another engine roared in the woods. "That's probably Hal and his brother," I told Garland. He glanced toward the distant sound. "Do they know what they're up against?"

I nodded. "I texted them. Arno's on his way too."

Shooting erupted in the distance. The shots pinged off metal, followed by a sharp cry of pain. I tensed, taking a step toward the growl of the incoming 4-wheeler.

A moment later, Hal's voice called out. "Joey?"

I expelled air in a relieved breath.

Mom and Garland shared a look. "Are you coming?" he asked my mom.

I reached out and took her gloved hand. "Mom, no. Stay with me."

She glanced at me, chewing her lip, and then nodded. "I'm sorry, Joey. I'll be in touch. We'll explain everything."

And, before I could form a plan to stop them, they were running away from me through the woods.

"Joey!" Hal came out of the trees on the river side as more gunfire erupted in the distance.

Instinctively, I ducked.

He reached me, pulling me into his arms. "Are you okay?"

"I'm fine." I looked toward the creek, to the spot where I'd last seen Medford and my mom. "But you're not going to believe what just happened."

"Hal?" Cal's voice dragged Hal's attention from me.

"Over here!"

Cal was pink-faced and running as he cut through the trees in our direction. He was wearing jeans and his leather coat, with a camo-design tactical vest over his coat. "We lost them. They got to the chopper before we could reach them in the ATVs."

Hal nodded. He didn't look surprised. "Whoever these guys are, they know what they're doing."

Cal slid a look over me. "Where's your mom?"

I pointed down the creek. "They went that way."

Hal's dark brows lifted. "They?"

The roar of more approaching ATVs cut in before I could explain. It was just as well. I didn't want to tell my story multiple times. I pointed to Arno roaring up on the lead all-terrain vehicle. No wonder it had taken him so long to arrive. They would have had to grab the trailer with the vehicles from the station garage before taking off.

Arno stopped his four-wheeler close to the guy bleeding into the snow and climbed off. "Is everybody okay?" He crouched next to the victim, feeling for the guy's pulse. "Who's the DB?"

Another deputy roared up behind Arno and stopped, cutting his noisy engine. I recognized Deputy Miller beneath the black *Deer Hollow Sheriff's Department* ball cap. He was a new deputy who'd relocated from the Indianapolis Metropolitan Police Department. He had a wife and two small children and had liked the relative quiet of a country situation. I wondered if he was currently rethinking that.

I watched Miller circle the body, cop eyes taking in the position, the obvious cause of death, and the surrounding area.

Belatedly responding to Arno's question, I shrugged. "I don't know. Garland Medford shot him."

Everyone stilled, all eyes on me.

I fought the urge to twitch under all that scrutiny. "Yeah, it's true. He's alive. And my mom just left with him. Willingly." I frowned. "I'd even say happily."

Hal's brows lifted in surprise. "She *wanted* to go with him?"

I nodded. "They wouldn't tell me what was going on. But I got the impression he had something to do with her being here."

Arno shoved his own cap back on his head. "Well, that's a kick in the shins."

"Yeah," I said, understanding the sentiment behind his words.

"And they just left you here?" Hal said in a too-soft tone.

My gaze jerked up to his. He was rigid, his pretty green eyes like two emeralds glittering in his face. I knew he was clenching his teeth by the little muscle that danced in his bristled jaw. "They tried to get me to go. But I told them you were coming. And then you called out to me. They took off."

Arno pointed down the creek and jerked his chin. "Miller, go. Don't confront Medford. He might get aggressive with Mrs. Fulle. Just locate and report back."

I stiffened at the idea of Medford hurting my mom. I still didn't trust him with her.

Nodding his understanding, the deputy climbed onto his ATV and took off in the direction Garland and my mother had gone.

Hal looked at Arno. "Did you get the FCC ID number on the chopper?"

Arno sighed. "Deliberately obscured. But I have a feeling it wouldn't tell us anything anyway. I'm going to dig into it when I get back to the station."

I shivered, my gaze falling on the last spot I'd seen my mom. My mind replayed everything she and Garland had said to me, trying to find a plausible story in the words.

I was so lost in my thoughts I didn't realize Hal was talking to me until he touched my arm. I jumped. "Oh! Sorry. What did you say?"

"Penny for your thoughts?" Hal gave me an understanding smile.

I shrugged. "I'm just having trouble wrapping my mind around all this."

"Understandable."

We watched Arno and Cal search the body in the snow.

"It's just..." I shoved my hands into the pockets of

my coat. "All this time, I've been worried about Medford hurting my mom. Now that's all upside down in my head. He saved her today. He saved *us*. And someone else was trying to kill us." I looked at Hal. "Why? Who? I'm flummoxed."

Hal nodded to the corpse in the snow. "Maybe the identity of the dead guy will tell us something."

Arno's cell rang. He pulled it out of his pocket and answered. "Deputy Willager." He listened for a moment, glanced at me, and then nodded. "Be right there."

My heart thundered in my chest. Had my mom been hurt? I took a step toward Arno as he stood. "What's happened? Is my mom okay?"

Arno slipped his phone into his pocket. "As far as I know, you're mom's fine. That was Deputy Sheppard. He and Schmidt have been canvassing the woods around where the chopper landed. They found someone."

Arno's eyes narrowed slightly. The way he was looking at me made me uncomfortable.

"Who is it?" Hal asked, stepping up beside me. His bulk and warmth were a comforting bulwark in a sea of icy fear.

"Don't know his identity yet. But he wants to talk."

I nodded. "That's good, right?"

Arno scrubbed a hand over his jaw, nodding. "It could be good. Except he'll only talk to you."

When we walked into the Sheriff's Office building, a petite, pretty woman jumped out of a hard chair and barreled toward me with a squeal. "Joey! Are you all right? Is it true? Did you see Gar..." Arno cleared his throat and Felly's lips snapped shut. She lowered her head and voice so none of the other people waiting to see one of the cops could hear. "You ran into Garland Medford?"

I sighed. "Unfortunately."

My cousin shook her head. "Only *you* could go for a walk in the woods and start an international war."

I frowned. "International?"

Arno cleared his throat again, giving my cousin the stink eye. "Oops." She made a zipping motion over her lips. "Sorry."

"Come on," Arno said, opening the door into the rest of the station. "You wait here, Felicity."

"Sure thing, Arno." She winked at me and stepped in behind me, grabbing the back of my coat and walking so close she plodded onto the back of my shoe with every other step. "Ouch. Ow. Ouch!" I murmured, getting back a whispered mantra of, "Oops, sorry, oops."

Arno turned with a frown as Felly deftly stepped

behind Hal, using his much bigger frame to hide her uninvited presence.

I stepped closer to Hal to help him hide her.

Arno eyed my boyfriend with suspicion.

Hal raised his hands. "What?"

As Arno turned away and headed toward the Interview rooms, Felly blew me a kiss and veered off toward the snack room, no doubt jonesing for a coffee.

Arno stopped in front of Interview Room B. He turned to me. "We'll be on the other side of the glass. He's cuffed to the table and at the ankles. He can't get to you."

Beside me, Hal stood stiffly, his body language screaming how much he didn't want me to go in there alone.

I nodded, chewing on my lip. "What do you want me to find out?"

"As much as you can," Arno told me unhelpfully. "But try to get names and find out what they were after. The firefight in the woods only makes sense if they were after your mother. Maybe our guy can tell us why they want Joline, what Garland's up to, and why the shootout."

"Is that all?" Hal asked with an unhappy grunt. "You're not asking for much."

Arno shrugged. "Anything she can get us will help."

Arno's cell rang. He looked at caller ID and

frowned, glancing up at Hal. "It's your buddy Pru Frect."

I tensed. Prudence Frect was Hal's too perfect, classy, over-confident friend with the FBI. She was Superwoman with looks, intelligence, grace, and style. And she had eyes for my boyfriend. Next to her, I felt like the ugly matron of honor at the Shrek wedding.

"Agent Frect, how can I help you?" Arno listened for a moment, and twin lines moved in between his brows. "You've got to be kidding me?"

He listened some more. His expression did not improve. "Are you people willing to risk losing track of Medford again?"

I could hear Pru's light, feminine voice on the other end of the line. But I couldn't make out what she was saying.

Judging by the murderous look on his face, Arno probably wished he couldn't hear her words either. "I'm not just flinging her into that room without eyes and ears. She's a civilian."

*Oh, oh.* I glanced at Hal. His expression had gone from tense to angry. I reached out and clasped his hand. He squeezed mine in his warm grip, but his gaze stayed locked on Arno.

"Fine. But I'm holding the FBI responsible if this goes badly."

I heard Pru trill a cheerful response and felt my teeth grinding together.

Hal was already shaking his head as Arno disconnected. "Not happening, Arno. She's not going in without at least visual backup."

"I agree. And she'll have that. Unfortunately, the bureau's insisting that the conversation not be audio or videotaped."

"Why?" I asked. Nothing was making any sense.

Arno shrugged. "Agent Frect says she'll be down in the morning to retrieve our prisoner. She said she'd tell us what she could then."

Hal crossed his arms over his chest. "I don't want Joey to go in there alone."

Arno looked at me. "I'm not wild about the idea either, Joey," he said. "It's up to you. If you don't want to talk to him, you don't have to."

I chewed the inside of my lip for a beat. I didn't want to talk to the man under any circumstances. Especially since Pru had put me in a particularly dicey spot. If I found out anything useful, I'd be the only one who heard the information directly. There'd be zero record. No proof of anything I repeated when I came out.

Which would make me a pretty big loose end for somebody. Then again, I needed to know what my mom was mixed up in.

That thought had me nodding. "I'll do it. But you'll still be behind the glass, right?"

Arno nodded.

Hal hesitated. "Given the new situation. I'm

standing by the door with an open line to you, Arno. If things start to get the least bit dicey, I'll be seconds away instead of minutes."

I nodded. I liked the idea of Hal being just on the other side of the door. "Okay." I ran my palms over my jeans to dry them.

Arno patted me on the shoulder and ducked into the observation room.

"Ready?" Hal asked.

I grimaced and then nodded. "Yes...no...maybe?"

He lifted his brows.

I reached for the knob. "Wish me luck."

"I'll be right here, honey."

Pulling air into my lungs to soothe my jangling nerves, I turned the knob and walked inside.

## 9

The man sitting at the table was looking down at his hands, his wrists cuffed and resting on the table. He appeared relaxed to the point that he was examining his nails.

He looked up slowly as I closed the door with a soft snick, leaning back against it.

The guy was almost too pretty for a man. Thick dark hair swept back from an unlined forehead, his warm olive-toned skin the color of a latte. The man's eyes were deep-set, the color a rich, mahogany brown. His nose was long, too perfect in the center of a face with high cheekbones, full lips, and a broad jawline. When he smiled, a dimple appeared in one cheek. If I hadn't known he and his friends had tried to kill my mom and me, I might have thought that dimple charming.

"Miss Joey Fulle."

I blinked, recognizing that smooth, slightly accented voice. It was the mask.

He motioned toward the chair across the table from him as if he were hosting a luncheon or asking me to tea. "Sit. Please."

"I don't think so. I can hear you just fine from here."

His smile slid away and he nodded. "I understand. You believe we are enemies, you and I."

My brows peaked and I fought a bitter laugh. "I wonder why. You break into my house, threaten my family, and then attack us on my property. Gee, why would I not trust you with my life?"

He looked down at his hands again, seeming thoughtful. He sighed. Apparently, my resistance to his charms aggrieved him. "I have not, nor will I ever allow your family to come to harm."

"Oh, well. When you put it like that, why wouldn't I believe you completely?"

His gaze rose to mine, locked on, and lit with intensity. "Because my...uncle would not allow it."

I fought to hide my surprise. "So, I was right. You *are* related to Garland."

The man inclined his chin. His speech patterns and movements felt very European. But as far as I knew, Garland Medford was American, born and raised. "He's worked very hard to keep you and your mother safe."

I forgot my determination to keep space between

us and suddenly found myself leaning over the table toward him, my palms pressing against the cool wood. I pinned him with a hostile glare. "He. Killed. My. Father." Actually, he'd paid someone to kill my father. Potato, potahto.

The man didn't deny it. He simply shook his head. "All is not as it seems. You do not understand."

I straightened, lifting my palms. "I'm here. Explain it to me."

"I wish I could, Joey. I truly do. But I cannot."

"Then tell me how a dead man has come to be resurrected."

"Good question. Let's just say the benefits of being dead no longer outweighed the detriments."

I scowled at him. "Do you write fortune cookie messages on the side?"

His laughter was soft and rich, reflected in his brown gaze. "Perhaps I should."

"Okay," I said. "If Garland isn't trying to kill us. And you're not trying to kill us, then who is? Are you working with him? You say you want to keep us safe. Tell me who's trying to kill us so we can protect ourselves."

He stared at me for a long moment. "The largest, most powerful rat in the sewer," he finally said.

I expelled a frustrated breath. "Rat, huh?"

He inclined his chin. "I'll admit you were in grave danger today. Your mother was not to be killed. Only taken. She has something someone needs. But once she provides it..." He lifted his cuffed hands, spreading the fingers and cocking his head. "If I tell you more, I will compromise every-thing." He glanced quickly at the mirror and then at me. Leaning forward, he spoke in a voice I could barely hear. "I am a pet mouse in a sewer filled with rabid rats." He extended his hands, palms out. He'd written something across the center of one of them. Three words. "Ask Prudence Frect," the tidy message read. He licked two fingers and rubbed at the ink, removing the message. "Take care who you share that information with, Miss Joey. Much danger lurks in the knowledge." And, with that overly dramatic statement, he turned his head and glanced toward the mirror, giving Arno a wave and a smug smile.

The insufferable man was dismissing me.

*Wonderful.* I thought. Just flipping wonderful. I was going to have to talk to little Miss Perfect to get my answers. I turned away without another word, happy to be released from the interview. I was so eager to leave that I nearly bowled Hal over as I dove through the door into the hallway.

O ur debrief of my little meeting didn't take long. I hadn't learned much.

"A pet mouse in a sewer full of rabid rats?" Arno repeated with a disbelieving look. "What the heck does that mean?"

I shrugged. "I was hoping you'd know."

"What else did he say?" Hal asked.

I carefully kept my expression neutral as I looked at him. "He insists that Garland is protecting mom and me."

"Do you believe him?" Arno asked.

"I have to at this point," I said. "My mother seems to trust the man. She clearly knows more than I do." I expelled a rush of frustrated air. "I wish somebody would fill me in." I shook my head, "He told me that those men today would have killed me if they'd gotten the chance. But that they would have taken my mom." My gaze found Hal's. "They think she has something and she's relatively safe until she gives it to them."

"Do you have any idea what she has?" Arno asked me.

"Not a clue."

We sat in silence for a moment, each of us lost in our own thoughts.

Hal finally broke the silence. "Did you find out anything about that chopper?" he asked Arno.

Arno nodded. "It was stolen," Arno said. "Whoever stole it snuck into a small airport twenty miles from Deer Hollow in the middle of the night and took it. The owner reported it missing a couple of hours ago when he went to perform maintenance." He picked up a sheet of paper and waggled in front of us. "And we just got an anonymous call that someone dumped a helicopter in the middle of a cornfield. How much do you want to bet it's the same chopper?"

Hal's phone dinged with a text. He slid it from his pocket. "Sure. I'll bet a hundred dollars that it's the same chopper."

Arno shook his head. "I'm not taking that bet."

Judging by my PI's expression, the text was not good news. "What's wrong?"

He shook his dark head. "I can't believe it. Their timing stinks."

"What?" I asked, dread making my pulse race. "Is it my mom? Are she and Garland at the house?"

I felt my pockets and realized I'd left my cell phone in Hal's car. Mom had probably been trying to reach me and gave up, reaching out to Hal instead.

"No." He gave me an apologetic smile. "I wish it was Joline. Unfortunately, my parents just showed up at my cabin. They heard Cal was here and thought it would be fun to visit since...and I quote... we never come visit them."

Arno chuckled. "Have fun with that. I'll let you

know if I get a bead on the person who's after Joey and Joline."

Cal's phone dinged as we approached the desk where he and Felly had plopped themselves. The desk was the one nearest the door, and there were no signs that it belonged to anybody. Felly waved as we entered the bullpen, a fat donut in one hand and a steaming mug of coffee in front of her on the desk.

"You look pretty comfy," I told my cousin, grinning.

She glanced behind me. "Deputy Grumpy's not coming out here, is he?"

I laughed. "You better hope not, if he catches you making yourself at home, he might put you to work filing stuff or cleaning the bathrooms." I borrowed Hal's phone and dialed my mom, hoping she'd answer my call. I was worried about her. And I was surprised she hadn't tried to contact me to make sure I was all right. It rang several times, and I disconnected.

Felly's perfectly sculpted brows rose into her hairline. "Girl, I've seen those bathrooms. I want nothing to do with that."

"We need to leave anyway," Cal said, looking grim. "Mom and dad are at the cabin."

Felly and I shared a look. Felly didn't look any happier about the news than I was.

Hal cocked his head at me, one dark brow rising. "You look thrilled."

I immediately felt guilty. It wasn't that I hated his parentals. They were actually very nice. But they just made me nervous. I didn't know why. "No. I'm good. Felly and I can spend the day at my house catching up with each other while you two see your parents."

Cal and Hal shared a laugh.

Cal grabbed the last bite of donut from Felly's fingers and stuffed it into his mouth. "Come on, Princess. My mom said she can't wait to see you."

Felly visibly deflated.

I looked at Hal. "I don't suppose your mom just wants to see Felly?"

Hal grabbed my hand and planted a kiss on the back of it. "She wants to talk about Esther Squeaks. Apparently, a friend of hers is considering getting a pot-bellied pig and you're just the person to talk to about it."

I did manage to keep my groan internal. Mostly. But it was close.

---

The navy blue Lexus sedan I recognized as belonging to the parental Amitys was parked in front of Hal's cabin. Cal's truck, a shiny black F150 pickup, was parked next to it. Hal and I had stopped for gas and to pick up a couple of bottles of wine on the way over, so Cal and Felly had been there a while when we arrived.

I twined my fingers nervously in my lap, wishing the cabin was further away from the drive as it had been when Hal had bought and renovated the old place. One of the improvements Hal had made was to bring in gravel and extend the drive all the way to the house.

*Dangit!*

Hal's big, warm hand landed on my twisting fingers. "They don't bite, honey."

"I know. I like them. A lot."

"Then why does seeing them make you such a nervous wreck?"

"I..." I swallowed a knot in my throat and sighed. "I have no idea."

"I know why." When I looked at him, he smiled. "Because you want them to like you."

And there it was. Simple. Obvious. Stupid. I winced. "What if they hate me?"

His chuckle warmed my belly and made me forget, for just a beat, that I was panicking. "They couldn't possibly hate you, Joey. You're kind and caring and beautiful." He waggled his brows at me.

I laughed. "I'm pretty sure your mom doesn't care what I look like."

He kissed the back of my hand. "Really? Well. That last part might have been me."

I laughed.

"Take a deep breath and stop worrying. Remember, Felly's been in there with them for a whole twenty minutes. She's probably fallen over three things by now, choked on her own spit and nearly burned the cabin down. Next to that train wreck, they're going to think you walk on water."

I spluttered out a laugh, watching him come around the big car to open the door for me. It was a bit of an exaggeration, but pretty close to true. I would have felt bad about his portrayal of my ditzy cousin, but she'd be the first to agree with it. Felly was comfortable and happy with who she was. I envied her that.

Hal handed me down from the SUV and enclosed my hand in a firm grip.

An icy wind cut through the trees and slashed at us. I yelped, tugging my coat close. Hal wrapped himself around me and pulled me close as we did an awkward, zombies on the warpath, kind of walk-shuffle to the door.

It flew open as Hal reached for it and Felly barreled out. "'Scuse me!" she screamed. Flames were licking skyward from a pan she held in front of her as she charged past to the edge of the tiny porch and pitched the flaming contents of the charred pan into the snow.

It hit with a thud and a sizzle, and she sagged against the railing, her small hands still covered in oven mitts. She glanced our way, her face lighting up. "Hey, you two."

"Hey," I said, a smile fighting for purchase on my lips. "What's up?"

"Nothing's up." She jerked her head toward the still sizzling pan. "The sloppy joes are definitely *down*, though. And I'm pretty sure that pan's a goner." She winced. "Sorry, Hal."

"No worries," he said, covering his mouth with his hand. "We can always go out to dinner."

And just like that, Felly's frown slid away. "Great idea! I'll tell Cal. He'll be relieved."

She hurried into the cabin ahead of us, calling to Cal.

Hal leaned close, his lips touching my ear as he whispered. "I told you so."

I shook my head. "It's like you can see the future."

We went inside, Hal chuckling.

The tiny cabin was toasty warm. A cheerful fire crackled in the big fireplace in the main living room. The room appeared empty until a dark head popped up on the other side of the couch that faced the fire.

Mrs. Amity's attractive face turned our way. "There you are. Is everything okay?"

I wondered if Cal and Felly had filled the parents in on what had happened in my woods earlier in the day.

Hal nodded. "Great. How's it going here?"

A happy squeal sounded from the other side of the couch at the sound of Hal's voice. Esther Squeals trotted around the furniture and ran to us, bumping our legs affectionately with her head.

I reached down and scratched the little thatch of hair between her big ears. "Hi, sweet girl. Are you having fun with our company?"

Esther Squeaks wiggled her nose and made piggy noises, and then trotted back around to Mrs. Amity. "She's adorable!" Hal's mom said. "We've been playing ball together, but now she's trying to steal my blanket from me." Her voice was filled with fond amusement. Her green eyes sparkled when she looked at me. "Hi, Joey. How are you?"

I waved like an idiot. "Hey. I'm great." I forced myself to leave Hal's comforting presence and walk around the couch. Mrs. Amity was sitting on the rug in front of the fire, her back pressed to the couch and her long legs stretched out in front of her. She was in her stocking feet and had a plaid fleece blanket spread half over her shins. Esther was head butting the blanket, trying to burrow under it as Mrs. Amity tugged on it playfully. "I never knew how much fun pigs could be," she told me, her eyes alight. "Asher hasn't stopped talking about Esther and Caphy and even that cat of yours." She shook her head. "I've never been a cat person myself, but I think I'd like LaLee's outlook on life."

I laughed. "Yeah, she's a force of nature."

Hal bent down and kissed the top of his mom's head. "I'm glad you're here."

She grabbed his hand and gave it a squeeze. "Me too, honey. I love what you've done to this place. I barely recognized it."

Hal couldn't hide his pleasure. "Thanks. I like it a lot."

"Hey, Son!" Mr. Amity called from the kitchen that Hal had built onto the side of the little cabin. The new, greatly updated kitchen was one of the additions Hal had made when he'd bought what had basically been a one-room house, with a tiny alcove on the back that the previous owner, my Uncle Dev, had called the bedroom. It had barely fit a single bed and the nightstand Dev used as a dresser. Dev had had a clothes rack instead of a closet that he crammed in behind the bed.

Hal had added a twelve hundred square foot addition to the house. The new section had included a good-sized master bedroom suite with a beautiful master bath, a walk-in closet, and the kitchen.

I watched Hal join Cal and his father in the kitchen. Cal handed his brother a beer and called out to me. "Wine? Or beer?"

I shook my head. "Nothing right now. Thanks."

Cal nodded and went back to cleaning up the mess Felly had made cooking.

"I understand your mom's here for a visit," Mrs.

Amity said. "Is she going to join us for dinner? I'd love to meet her."

Without warning, tears sprang to my eyes.

Hal's mom looked alarmed. "Oh. Did I say something wrong? I'm sorry."

I sniffed, scraped the heels of my hands over my suddenly wet cheeks, and shook my head. "No. It's fine. I'm just..." Words escaped me. I didn't know what Cal and Hal had told their parents, if anything, about my situation. And I didn't want to open up a can of worms. "She's...um...I lost her."

Mrs. Amity's eyes went wide. "Lost? Oh, honey..."

Too late, I realized that I'd given the wrong impression. "No!" The word ejected from my mouth with too much force, shocking everyone. Mrs. Amity paled, her lips forming an "O" of surprise. All conversation in the kitchen stopped. I turned to flap my hand at Hal, seeing him starting toward me. "Sorry, sorry...It's all good."

Embarrassment colored my face. I forced myself to look at Mrs. Amity. "I'm so sorry. My mom's not dead..." I blanched at the word. "She just had to leave early."

"Oh." I could tell Hal's mom wanted to ask more questions, but she was probably afraid of how I'd react.

I caught myself sliding further down into the couch, my face burning. No wonder I'd been afraid to spend time with Hal's parents. I was an idiot.

Suddenly, I couldn't stand the silence anymore. "So...sloppy joes, huh?" I said a mental apology to Felly for using her screwup to get myself out of an uncomfortable spot. I'd bake her cookies later to make up for it.

Mrs. Amity pressed her lips together. "I might have mentioned that they were a favorite. Felly's just not used to Hal's stove."

I nodded, trying to keep my expression neutral. "Yeah. I'm sure that' s it," I lied. My cousin had lots of great qualities, but cooking wasn't one of them. And she rarely had to clean up after herself. She'd lived a charmed life as a spoiled little rich girl in Indianapolis until her father had gotten into legal trouble and found himself running for his life from the Russian mob.

Felly and Cal had gone after him, finding him down south somewhere, living with a group of monks on the bayou. The stories she'd told us of the experience had made my stomach hurt from laughter.

With the money her dad had put into a trust for her, Felly still lived like a princess, but I thought the experience had brought her down to earth and made her more relatable.

Unfortunately, it hadn't done a thing for her cooking.

Speak of the devil. The door to the hall bathroom opened, and Felly came out. She was smoothing a bandage on her pinkie finger, frowning.

"Did you burn yourself?" I asked my cousin.

"She had quite the fire going there for a minute," Mrs. Amity told me, her lips twitching. At that moment, she reminded me of Hal trying to hide a smile.

"Who knew hamburger could burn like that," Felly said with a shrug. She dropped into the recliner near the fireplace. It was one of the things I loved most about Felly. She didn't beat herself up over stuff.

I could learn a lot from her on that subject.

Hal's mom patted the fat mound beneath the blankets, her expression happy. The bump under the fleece shifted once, a twisty tail briefly spinning near the edge, and then Esther Squeaks settled down for a nap.

Mrs. Amity leaned her head back on the couch and sighed. "This is very cozy. I can see why Hal loves it here."

Felly and I shared a look. Hal's and Cal's parents weren't wealthy, really, but they were comfortable. They'd always lived in a nice home in a gated community in the Indianapolis suburbs. Though his mom was sitting on the floor, snuggling with a pig, she was dressed in a soft, pale green sweater that I was pretty sure was angora, and her slender legs were covered in perfectly tailored black slacks.

The last time the Amity parentals had come to Deer Hollow, they'd pretty much declared the woods around Hal's cabin to be the equivalent of the Black Forest in the Grimm's Fairytales.

They'd been there to dump their youngest son, Asher, with Hal for some tough love. But, even though Asher had earned himself a temporary bivouac with his take-no-prisoners older brother, they hadn't felt comfortable leaving him at the cabin.

They'd brought the teenaged rascal to my house instead.

Good times.

"Mrs. Amity, how's my buddy, Asher?" I asked Hal's mom.

She opened her eyes and gave me a polite frown. "Call me Jennifer, please. You're making me feel ancient with that Mrs. Amity stuff."

I gave her an apologetic smile, nodding.

"Ash is doing really well." She shifted slightly in my direction, fixing me with a serious look that made my palms sweat. "I don't think we ever properly thanked you for helping Hal clear his brother. And for letting Asher share your home and your furry babies for a while." Unshed tears made Mrs... Jennifer's...green eyes sparkle like emeralds. "He came back to us a different young man."

"Different in a good way, I hope?"

Jennifer nodded. "Definitely. He's kinder and more considerate." She grinned. "I think his new girlfriend has something to do with that too. She's a doll."

"Girlfriend?" Felly asked.

I nodded. "He's dating Lis's cousin, Amethyst."

Felly's eyes went wide. "How'd that happen?"

"Ame just happened to be visiting Lis for the summer when Asher was here. They really hit it off."

"Yeah, Ame's great." Felly seemed like she would have said something else if her boyfriend's mom hadn't been sitting there. "I was hoping to see Lis while I was here."

"Yeah. She's in Nashville for a Realtor's convention. She's going to be mad she missed you. You'll just have to come back."

"Deal," Felly said.

Mr. Amity came into the room, sans his beer. Hal and Cal started grabbing coats and keys. "Okay, ladies, if everyone agrees, we've decided we'd like to hit that new barbeque place up the highway. It's about halfway to Indy, so it's right on our way home."

"Great!" Felly said, jumping out of the recliner. "I'm starving."

D inner was fun. Felly and Mr. Amity, or Dale, as he insisted Felly and I call him, were a hoot together. They seemed compelled to one-up each other in the wild story department and, between Felly's antics on the bayou and Dale's stories about the trouble his boys got into growing up, I could honestly say I'd never laughed so hard in my life.

Watching Hal and Cal squirm only added to the fun.

I'd also discovered where Hal had gotten his smile and kind eyes and who he'd inherited his dry sense of humor from.

I was feeling pleasantly tired and relaxed when Hal pulled into my drive.

It didn't last.

There was a car in my driveway that I didn't

recognize. It was a plain white sedan with North Carolina plates. My stomach tightened at the sight.

A man straightened from the front porch swing and walked to the steps, hands jammed into the pockets of his jeans. As he came into the light, my tension climbed another notch.

In the back seat where she'd just seconds ago been literally snoring, Felly sat bolt upright. "Who's that?" She squinted. "Wait. Is that…"

I sighed. "Yeah. It is."

"Who is it?" Cal asked. I twisted around to find him pulling a gun from under his short leather jacket.

"Joey's uncle."

I opened my mouth to deny the uncle part. After all, Dev was only an uncle in name. He and my dad had been best friends since grade school and, when my dad had been killed, Devon Little had taken it on himself to keep my mom and me safe. Mostly my mom, really, since she was the only one who seemed to be in danger. Though, when he and I had reconnected a little over a year earlier, it was because Dev had been checking up on me.

Devon Little was waiting on the porch, his expression grave.

Hal cut the engine, and we sat there for a beat while I worked up the energy to talk to the man on the porch.

"Are you up for this?" Hal asked, his voice filled with concern.

"I don't really have much choice," I said petulantly. Then I sighed, reaching for his hand. "Sorry. It's just..."

Hal nodded. "I know."

I avoided Devon's gaze as I cut the distance between us. I had no idea how I was going to explain my mother's desertion to him. I really didn't even understand their relationship. At one time, I'd believed they were just friends. But when they'd visited the previous Christmas, I'd gotten a different vibe from them. And the look on Devon's face told me he had strong feelings for my mom. Whether she shared them or not.

"Hey," I told my visitor.

"Hey, Joey. You look well." He skimmed a look over Felly and Cal, nodding.

Hal offered Devon his hand. "Mr. Little. It's nice to see you again."

"Dev, please," Devon insisted.

Cal stepped forward and Dev took his hand too. "Cal Amity, sir. It's a pleasure."

Felly squealed and ran into Devon's open arms, making him laugh. "You haven't changed a bit, young lady."

Felly pulled back, flushing in pleasure. "Well, *you* have," she said, playfully waggling her brows. "Hubba."

Devon threw back his head and laughed in a way I hadn't heard him laugh for years.

Inside the house, Caphy threw herself at the door and whined pitifully.

Dev's brows lifted. "Poor girl's been doing that for a half-hour. It's good you came home. I was starting to worry she'd hurt herself."

I quickly opened the door and Caphy flew out, eyes wide and tail whipping. Hal held up a hand and she screeched to a halt, dropping to her quivering butt in front of him.

My mouth fell open. Especially when Hal reached into the pocket of his coat and pulled out a tiny treat for her.

"What just happened?" I asked my boyfriend.

Cal laughed. "He's always been something of a dog whisperer. He can train anything."

"Almost anything," Hal corrected.

Cal stared at him for a beat and then laughed. "Oh yeah. BB." To us, he said, "We had a goofy little dog when we were kids. Long black and white hair and a cute little smushed face. Looked like a bedroom slipper..."

"Shi Tzu," Hal clarified. "Her name was Bonnie Bell. Sweet. But dumb as a bag of hair."

Cal nodded enthusiastically. "BB was mom's dog, and they adored each other. But the dog was untrainable."

Hal laughed. "Mom took her to obedience

training once. She couldn't even get the dog to walk on a leash."

"BB just laid down on the floor and quivered. Mom had to basically drag her around the circle until they came to the wall, then the dog would lean over and slide along the baseboard rather than walk."

We all laughed.

"Needless to say, BB flunked puppy class," Cal reported. "The trainer told mom she might need *special* training."

"A nice way to say she was untrainable," Hal said, laughing.

Caphy seemed to have taken our laughter as a release and was standing on her back legs, trying to reach Dev's face with her long tongue. He grinned at her, scratching her under the chin. "Hi, pretty girl. I missed you too."

"Shall we go in?" I asked, "It's cold out here."

Caphy took off at full speed and did zoomies around the yard as we headed inside.

"Coffee?" I asked Dev.

He shook his head. "No. But thanks. I stopped for dinner on the way here."

With a look from Hal, Cal and Felly excused themselves and went into the living room to watch TV.

I headed into the kitchen for a glass of water. Hal let Caphy inside. My pibl did a drive-by licking and then left us for the comfy warmth of snuggling with Felly and Cal.

Dev stood in the center of my kitchen, looking around. His etched but attractive face was filled with sadness. "Being in this house always brings back so many memories."

I nodded, settling a glass of water in front of him before sitting down with my own. Hal leaned against the sink, arms crossed over his chest. "You heard Garland's alive?" my PI asked Dev.

Devon nodded. "I did. Actually, I've known it for a while."

My brows climbed into my hairline. "And you didn't tell me?"

Devon looked startled as if he hadn't considered I might need to know. "I'm sorry, honey. It didn't occur to me." He sighed. "I guess I've been kind of wrapped up in the drama that is...has been...our lives, Joline and mine. I realize that was thoughtless." He dropped his head in his hands, suddenly looking exhausted. "I just seem to step in it no matter where I turn."

"Tell us what's going on, Dev," Hal said in a low voice. "Joey's been dropped right into the middle of this mess, and she has a right to know."

After a moment, Devon lifted his head and nodded. "You're right. I can't tell you everything..."

I bristled, angry heat flooding into my face.

Devon held up a hand. "Don't get your bloomers

in a twist, Joey. I recognize that look from your mother. Heaven knows I've seen enough of it lately. It's a wonder I'm not bloodied and bruised from all the rage she's been nurturing over the last month."

I unclenched my teeth and sipped some water. He was right. I needed to hear him out before I got my back up.

After that, I would hit him about the head and shoulders for leaving me to find my own way through a maze he'd apparently helped to build.

"Talk," I told my godfather.

He sipped his water, and I couldn't help feeling like he was stalling. But he didn't stall for long. Setting it down on the counter, he wrapped his fingers around it and stared off into the distance, his gaze unfocused. "We've always believed someone in Garland's organization had your father killed. We thought it was because of the money Sasha had with her that night. We assumed she'd stolen it from Medford Industries."

Sasha Gardner had been Garland Medford's girl-friend, who'd apparently taken some money from Medford and had come to my parents, asking them to use their prodigious distribution network to get her safely away. I was vague on the details of why my parents would have gotten involved. But I'd assumed Sasha had been charming or persuasive enough to convince my father she was a victim deserving of his help despite the danger involved.

Or she'd offered him enough money to make it worth his while.

Maybe my mother had been right about my father falling for Sasha. Though I still had trouble believing it.

"Even when we learned about the Johnstons' part in the murders, I thought Medford had hired them for the job."

Belle and Edward Johnston had lived in Deer Hollow for decades before we learned the older couple had been leading a shadow existence as assassins for hire. It had taken them trying to finish the job of killing my mom, using me as bait, for the Feds to finally put Belle in jail. Unfortunately, her predatory husband had gotten away to kill another day.

"—and with Edward still out there..."

"You believed Mom still wasn't safe." I nodded impatiently. "I know all that. Tell me something I don't already know."

Dev waited out my mini-tantrum before going on. "It was complicated, but we thought Medford was behind everything. At least, I always believed that. I know now that we were meant to think that..."

"He wasn't?" Hal asked, frowning.

"No." Devon took a breath. "He's been working for the Feds all this time."

My stomach twisted. Everything I thought I'd known was wrong. "But why? And how is mom involved?" I thought about how Garland had embraced my mother. How she'd leaned into him. They were involved. I'd bet my house on it.

But where did that leave Devon?

"Sasha Gardner was a confidential informant for the feds. She was burned. When Medford realized the man he was tracking knew Sasha was a CI, he tried to get her safely away."

"So he's the money and power behind The Fulle's assignment to move her to safety," Hal said, putting the pieces together.

"He was the money. But not the power. Someone at the FBI is running that show. And I don't know who it is." Devon narrowed his gaze at me. "Did your mother say anything, Joey? Does she know who's behind the sting at the FBI?"

I thought about what Garland's nephew had said. If he *was* Garland's nephew. At that point, I didn't believe anybody. "She didn't tell me anything." That wasn't a lie, at least. *She* hadn't.

I glanced at Hal and caught him staring at me, a speculative look in his eye. He knew me too well.

"So, why now?" Hal asked. "Why did Medford fake his own death? And why resurrect himself now?"

A sense of déjà vu slid through me at Hal's question, so similar to mine. But the answer Devon gave him was not at all similar to the one Garland's nephew gave me.

"Because something has happened that endangers all the players trying to bring the target down. Somebody talked. Somebody who should have been on the good guys' side. And I'm guessing it was whoever is running this operation for the FBI."

## 11

I fought the urge to cringe. "You think someone in the FBI is dirty?" I asked.

Devon shrugged. "How else could this have happened? Medford's definitely been burned. His people have too. And somebody knew about your mother."

I felt Hal's assessing gaze on me and forced myself not to look his way. "Devon, it's long past time you told me what mom is involved in. Obviously, somebody thinks she knows something she shouldn't. What is it?"

Devon idly spun the glass of water in front of him, his brows lowered over an unreadable gaze. He finally sighed. "All I know is what your dad told me before he was killed. When he knew they'd be relocating Sasha. If he knew what he was talking about, then someone thought Sasha had a piece of very incriminating evidence against somebody with a lot of money and a long reach."

Hal shifted closer as if trying to protect me. "Who's the target?" he asked.

That was the difference between my PI and me. My first question was, "What do they think she has?"

Devon looked from me to Hal. "Your guess is as good as mine on the who. The what...?" He shook his head. "Sasha carried more than money away on the plane that night. She had a recording too. Apparently, she overheard and recorded a phone call the night before she ran. There was supposedly some incriminating information on the call, having to do with some murders."

My brows lifted. "Murders?"

"Yeah. It's as bad as it sounds. The victims were apparently killed for crimes against our powerbroker, whoever that is. Sasha couldn't recognize the target's voice on the recording. But she knew that the fed's targeted amplification equipment could isolate and pinpoint the speaker, leading them to the target."

"If Sasha Gardner had the recording with her, why wouldn't this target assume it was destroyed in the crash and resulting fire?" Hal asked.

"Or taken by Edward Johnston when he presumably took the money," I suggested. We'd been operating on the assumption that my father's killer had waited until after the crash and then retrieved the briefcase full of cash Sasha had left Indianapolis with before the police arrived. We hadn't known about any recording. But it made sense Johnston would have known about it.

Devon shrugged. "It would certainly be great leverage for someone unscrupulous to use against the Target," he agreed. "Unfortunately, Johnston was very good at hiding his own tracks and pointing the finger at Joline. Now, he's in the wind and she's still in danger."

Depression pressed down on me like a lead weight. I'd been right to worry that my mom was still in danger. But somewhere deep inside, I'd hoped I was wrong. "She was safe where she was," I said, tears burning my eyes. "Why didn't she just stay there?"

Devon didn't respond. His silence felt unnatural. He hadn't even asked where she was. I lifted my gaze to his. "What happened, Devon?"

"I messed up, Joey." He stared at the floor for a beat. Then, with a sigh, he lifted his gaze to mine. "I told her I loved her."

I closed my eyes against the pain in his face.

He sniffed, scrubbing at his cheeks. "She didn't want to hear it. I'd always suspected she loved him. They'd been together years ago before she met your father, but life had taken them in separate directions. Still, she was noticeably animated when we learned he might still be alive. Soon after that, she started being more withdrawn and I suspected she was keeping things from me. We were drawing apart, but I didn't want to admit it to myself." He sighed. "Being together these last couple of years, sharing the same fears and living on the front edge of a storm..." He took a long, shaky breath. "I'd hoped we'd built something. But...she never thought of me that way. We were friends. And now I've ruined even that."

I reached out and grasped his hand. "I'm so sorry."

He squeezed my fingers. His hand was rough and cold. "No. Don't be. She never lied to me. I did this to myself."

"You can't control who you love," I told him. "You gave up everything for her."

"Because I made your dad a promise. I don't regret a minute of it."

Neither of us spoke for a minute. Finally, Devon lifted his head, his eyes clear of tears. "She's with Medford?"

My instinct was to lie. But he'd been honest with me. I owed him the same back. "Yeah. We were attacked in the woods. Garland showed up and..." I shook my head. "I didn't trust him. But she...left with him." I thought about my fears. My doubts. "Do you think he could be using her to find this recording? Is it possible he's not who he says he is?"

Devon seemed to consider my question. He

finally grimaced. "It's possible. But if you're asking me if I believe it, the answer is no. I believe he loves her. I believe he always has. It's probably why he never married."

I wasn't sure if what he said made me feel better or worse.

My doubts must have shown on my face because he added, "If anybody can keep her safe from these people, Medford can."

I shook my head, words lost to me. Everything I'd believed for years was wrong. I was living in opposite world.

Except for the most important thing. That was still true.

My mom was still in terrible danger.

Devon stood up. "I'm going. If you need me, call. Otherwise, I'll do my best to lay down an alternate trail. Maybe they'll follow it thinking she's still with me. It will buy her some time."

On an impulse, I stood up and threw my arms around his neck like I had as a little girl. I held on tight for a long moment, only stepping back when he pulled away.

Devon tapped me on the tip of my nose like he had when I was a child. "You take care, Miss Joey. My guess is that Medford has eyes on you, and he'll keep you safe. But don't take any unnecessary risks."

I thought of the guy at the Sheriff's station.

Could he be Garland's eyes on me? I nodded. "I won't. You take care of yourself too."

He shook Hal's hand and walked out. I stood in front of the living room window, watching him drive away. My throat was clogged with tears. My bones felt heavy.

Hal came up behind me and wrapped his arms around me, not speaking as Devon's rented car eased its way down the drive.

Behind us, the television played on. Cal and Felly were silent, but I knew they weren't watching it. I wondered what they were thinking.

A warm weight pressed against my thigh. I looked down to find Caphy staring up at me. She whined softly. "Hey, pretty girl."

Hal scratched her ears. "What do you want to do?" he asked softly.

I wished I knew. I shook my head, suddenly feeling so tired. "I'm going to bed. It's been a long day."

He squeezed my shoulders and I turned away, heading for the stairs.

"Night," Felly said, her voice soft.

I lifted a hand but didn't turn. "See you in the morning."

Caphy followed me up. LaLee yowled when we came into my bedroom. She stood, arching her back in a leisurely stretch, and then resettled herself in the center of her pillow.

I pulled off my clothes and slipped on boxers and a tee, brushed my teeth, and climbed into bed. Caphy jumped up too and stretched alongside me, ignoring the scolding she received from the cat.

I lay there knowing I'd never get to sleep. Not with everything spinning through my mind.

I was wrong. Sometime later, I started to drift away. And just before I fell completely into sleep, I remembered I hadn't told Hal what I knew about Pru.

---

Dancing elephants.

Dancing. Elephants.

I winced at the thunderous sound of their big feet, twitching when each concussive connection made the giant circus lights flicker.

An elephant broke from the ring, panicked and trumpeting wildly as a small white mouse chased it into the crowd.

Right at me.

I screamed, backtracking as fast as I could as people scattered away from me in sheer terror. I knew I should turn and run. But something told me it wasn't a good idea to turn away from the rampaging elephant. Its eyes were glowing, a terrifying, demonic red glow that skittered ice along my spine.

The elephant's enormous feet boomed, the lights flickered, people screamed and ran.

Backtracking at an ankle-risking speed, I slammed into something hard and immovable.

A wall.

Somewhere in the distance, bells rang.

*Ring. Ring. Ring.*

The mouse stopped suddenly. It cocked its little white head with its tiny paws folded in front of it and seemed to frown.

Boom, boom, boom. Ring. Ring. Ring.

Boom. Ring. Boom.

"Aren't you going to answer that?" the mouse asked with a straight face.

The elephant skidded to a stop close to me. So close. And lifted onto its hind legs, trumpeting as its evil red eyes flashed with rage.

Ring.

"Really, Joey," the mouse said. "What about your Pavlovian response?"

Ring.

Jerking upright in bed with a gasp, I looked around my bedroom but saw nothing to worry about there. It was dark and empty. I cast a glance toward the other pillow, seeing the tidy oval of LaLee still deeply asleep.

She wasn't worried about anything.

I relaxed. It was just a bad dream.

I fought the covers, suddenly thirsty. I'd go get a drink and then go back to sleep.

Grimacing, I tried to shove the covers away. My feet and legs stuck to the damp cotton and confounded my efforts. My red-blonde locks were a tangled mess that fell over my face, half obscuring my vision. I quickly shoved hair off my face and glanced at the cell phone on my bedside table. It vibrated insistently, its lighted face bright in the darkness.

Another light speared through the room. I jumped when I saw the shape perched on my window seat. Lightning flared around Caphy, painting her with a ghostly halo.

She didn't turn as I expelled a breath.

It was a storm. Caphy had always been fascinated by them. It wasn't unusual to find her watching one through a window.

But there was something discomfiting about the level of her interest.

*Boom!*

I jumped as thunder reverberated through the house, so powerful the glass in the windows rattled. Caphy shifted with the sound but never looked away from the chaos beyond the glass. It wasn't just the storm that had her transfixed. It was something else. "What is it, girl?" I asked. "What's wrong?"

Caphy whined, but she didn't turn away.

The phone on my nightstand started to vibrate

again. I didn't recognize the number. I remembered shutting off the ringer before I'd gone to bed. Yet, my dream had transformed the vibrations into rings.

But what was with the elephant? Booming feet probably equaled thunder, I told myself, answering my own question. The flickering lights would be the lightning. I didn't even want to think about that white mouse. I shivered. Heaven save me from an overactive imagination.

*Boom!*

Caphy quivered, pressing against the cushions as if they could protect her from the storm. Still, she didn't leave the window.

Carrying my phone with me, I climbed out of bed and padded barefoot to the window, dropping onto the seat behind my dog.

She briefly looked up at me, her pretty green eyes sparking in the distant lightning flash. The thunder hit again, but it was softer.

The storm was moving on.

"Stupid Indiana weather," I mumbled against my vibrating dog. Snow and ice yesterday. A thunderstorm today.

In some part of my brain, I'd known there was a warm front coming through, and the temperature swing was expected to be dramatic. Enough to bring on a storm.

The ground outside was a sea of glossy mush, the rain and snow mixing to create a dirty gray glaze that would, hopefully, capitulate to the sun in the morning.

I wrapped my arms around Caphy and lay my head against hers.

Her tail gave a single, welcoming swipe.

"What are you looking at, pretty girl?"

Caphy whined softly and gave my cheek a wet swipe with her tongue. But her gaze quickly returned to the window. Something in the yard had certainly grabbed her attention.

I leaned closer to the glass and peered into the darkness. The sky was cloudy and gray, which meant there was very little light out there. There were no streetlights where I lived. Not many headlights even came along the road.

Most of my exterior illumination, other than the spotlights on the house, came from the stars.

When the night was clear, billions of stars hung, bright and twinkling, above Deer Hollow. And the moon seemed close enough to touch. But it wasn't a clear night. Far from it. Which meant I was dependent on the occasional flash of lightning to show me what Caphy was looking at.

I could go down and turn on the exterior lights. But if I woke Hal I'd have to explain what I was doing. He'd go out there and probably get electrocuted, and I'd have guilt and sadness for the rest of my life.

I sighed again. "You're making me a nervous

wreck," I told the pibl. She wagged her tail again. "I'm going back to bed. Come on, girl."

Caphy whined.

Thunder boomed.

Lightning flared.

And my world upended.

A lone figure stood on the grass below my window. Staring up at me.

## 12

I didn't even think. I just started running. I hit the stairs in my bare feet and flew down them in the low light, nearly missing a step in the middle and skidding down on my heels before catching myself on the railing.

My heart pounded, but I couldn't seem to stop my feet from moving toward the front door. I fumbled with the locks, swearing softly under my breath as Caphy head-butted the back of my calves.

I wrenched the door open and raced out the door. My feet hit ice on the porch, I nearly went down again. I grappled with the railing and found it icy too.

Hal called my name, his voice filled with alarm. I kept running. Caphy shot past me and skidded over the icy concrete at the bottom of the steps, regaining traction as her claws found the sloppy grass. She tore across the yard, directly to the spot where I'd see the figure in the flash of distant electricity.

I slid along the concrete, feeling a bare patch abrade my flesh before I hit the grass.

Hal screamed my name again.

I barely heard him. I had tunnel vision for that one spot in the yard. My mind was locked on. My breath hitched and caught in my throat.

Ahead of me, Caphy had stopped and was circling the area, nose to the ground and tail wagging. Ice and rain splashed up around my bare legs. My feet ached from the cold. Icy rain dripped from my hair into my eyes, mixing with the tears.

Heavy footsteps sloshed up behind me. Strong hands grabbed hold of me, wrenching me to a stop. "No!" I screamed, my fingers digging into his, trying to get free. "Let me go! He's here. Let me go."

Hal wrenched me backward, up against his warm body. I screamed, fighting against him. "No! Please! I have to..." I couldn't finish the thought. I didn't know what I needed to do. The yard was empty. The figure I'd seen standing there, looking exactly like I remembered him, was gone.

I dissolved into tears. "I have to talk to him."

Hal turned me in his arms and reeled me in. "It's okay, honey," he said into my ear. Rain pelted us. The icy slush covering my feet burned against my skin. And I sobbed against Hal's shirt. I had no excuse for my behavior, except for the years of grieving. The months of fear since learning my mother was alive. The endless hours of wishing I'd had more time.

"Come on, Joey. Let's get you inside."

I shook my head. "He's here. I need to find him."

"Nobody's here, honey. Did you have a bad dream?"

*Yes!* But I was awake now. "It wasn't a dream. Caphy saw him too."

"Saw who?" Hal asked, his voice rough with emotion against the driving rain.

"I saw him," I said, my voice losing confidence. "He was right there."

Hal scooped me up into his arms. "You can tell me when we get inside." He whistled for Caphy. A moment later, she bounded past us to the house.

Hope plummeted.

He was gone. If he wasn't, Caphy would have kept looking for him.

Felly met us at the door. She tugged a sweater close around her as Hal carried me through the door. "Is she okay?" my cousin asked.

"She's freezing. Can you get her a heated blanket and something warm to wear?"

Felly spun on her heels and started running.

"Heavy socks," Hal yelled after her.

He settled me on the couch, wrapping himself around me until Felly returned. Then he moved away to give me privacy. "I'll fix hot chocolate," he said, leaving me to Felly's tender care.

---

The cold was invasive, burrowing into my bones and causing violent shaking I thought would never stop. Felly had hit the button to turn on the gas fireplace, and heat radiated from the fire, painting the air with warmth that didn't quite seem to reach me.

I shuddered under the knitted throw from the back of the couch, my feet stuffed into wool socks and slippers and my body encased in fleece.

I should have been sweating in the warm house. But the shock to my system had sucked the warmth from me just as seeing my dead father standing on the lawn had made me question my sanity.

"Are you sure it was him?" Felly asked in a quiet voice. She'd been treating me like I was a deranged person since Hal had carried me back inside, drenched and half-frozen. "It's really dark out there."

"Caphy and I both saw him. If it wasn't him, then who was it?" I asked her in my most reasonable voice. Unfortunately, my clanking teeth probably robbed the question of some of its power.

She shrugged. "It was only a quick flash of light," she said. "You were still half asleep. Maybe it was just a shadow."

The front door opened and closed again. Hal pulled off his jacket and boots, leaving them on the rug to dry. He ran strong fingers through his dark hair, scooping it straight back from his face. When he looked up at us, his expression was grim.

I turned to face him as he joined us. "What did you find?"

He glanced at Felly and then back to me. "Footprints. You didn't imagine it. Somebody was out there."

I sank back into the couch, my shoulders rounding. "I knew it."

Hal sat down beside me. He tucked a strand of my still-damp hair behind my ear. "Tell me what you saw, honey."

Down at my feet, Caphy stirred, her smooshy face turned up to me as if willing me to tell our tale. I smiled. She'd been my staunchest supporter and closest friend since I lost my parents. She'd been with me through everything and had never judged me. When she'd seen my father standing in our yard, she hadn't even barked. It was like she'd recognized him. Her conviction, more than anything, told me I wasn't crazy.

I turned to Hal, tears blurring the vision of his handsome face. "It was him, Hal. My father. How can he be here? Is everything a lie? I don't know what to believe anymore."

Hal pulled me against him, placing his chin on

top of my head. "There's truth in this somewhere," he said. "We're going to find it, honey."

I nodded, sniffling.

Caphy rose from the floor and placed her heavy head on my legs. I reached down and scratched her under the chin. "I know. It was just a shock."

"I can imagine."

Soft footfalls moved away from us toward the stairs. Felly was leaving us alone to talk.

In the distance, I heard a soft sound—a muted rumble.

It took a beat before my brain placed the sound. When it did, I jerked upright and stood so suddenly Caphy yelped in surprise.

I ran for the stairs, taking them two at a time. Hal's heavy steps and Caphy's nails clattering on the wood floor followed me up.

Felly was coming out of my room as I reached the top. She was holding my cell phone. "I heard this and, given the time of night, thought it might be important."

I grabbed it away from her and hit the button to answer the call. "Who is this?"

Silence pulsed through the line long enough for me to think the caller had hung up. Then a soft voice said. "Your mother hid something there. You need to find it and bring it to me, or everyone you love is going to die."

The call disconnected before I could respond.

And I sank to my knees on the rug as fear zapped strength from my legs.

Hal grabbed me under the arms. "Who was that?"

I quickly dialed my mom, listening to it ring. I gave up after the eighth ring. "I don't know." I shook my head. "He said mom hid something here and that I needed to bring it to him or everybody I loved would die." I lifted my gaze to Hal's, blinking back the last of my tears.

I shoved to my feet. Anger flared through me. I was done crying. I needed to get to the bottom of whatever was going on. I was sick of being used like some kind of hapless pawn.

Hal pulled out his cell and dialed. "Arno. I need you to find this phone." He rattled off the number while I ran toward the room my mother had used while she was there.

Felly's soft footfalls followed me. "What are we looking for?" she asked, without hesitation. "Where do you want me to look?"

I thought about it for a beat, trying to think like my mom. Where would she have hidden the recording? "I think we're looking for a memory stick. We need to search her room. If we don't find it there, we'll consider next steps."

I already knew where she probably hid it. But just to be sure, I'd make quick work of her room.

Felly and I walked into my old room, and I jolted

to a stop. The room looked like it had been tossed. Had my mom made that mess? Or had someone been inside my house while she and I were walking? Could they have? I turned to Felly. "While Mom and I were in the woods, where were you, Cal, and Hal?"

Felly flushed. "After we got back from the grocery. The boys went to the cabin to do some work. I used the tanning bed in the basement. I hope you don't mind? Cal's been promising to take me somewhere for a beach vacation. I was trying to get rid of my pasty winter skin."

The house had been empty. It would have been easy for the guys in the chopper to come inside. What was terrifying was that they'd only tossed the room where mom was staying. How had they known? I rubbed my arms, suddenly feeling exposed and vulnerable in my own home.

*What were we up against?*

I shook it off. "Will you go through the closet? Open everything, check every shoe, search every pocket. Take everything off the shelves and check those."

Felly nodded and went to work.

I checked all my favorite childhood hiding spots first, and then tackled the dressers, searching every drawer inside and out. When Hal came in, he pulled the bed apart to make sure there was nothing hidden there.

I even got down on my hands and knees and checked the edges of the carpet.

We came up empty.

By the time we walked out of mom's room, the sun was coming up.

I looked at Hal. "Have you heard back from Arno?"

"Not yet. I'm afraid the caller used a burner phone. Arno might not be able to trace it. He said if he needed to, he'd call Pru. The feds have better resources than he does."

All the blood rushed from my face and I winced.

"What?" Hal asked. "Why do I get the feeling you've been hiding something from me?"

I shook my head. "Not on purpose. But things keep happening, and I haven't had time."

Hal's expression softened. "Tell me."

"During the interview with that guy who Arno was holding..." I stopped, blinking. "Is he still holding him?"

"Unfortunately, no. The Sheriff bowed to political pressure and had to let him go."

"Political pressure from whom?" I asked.

"Feds, I think. I haven't really had a chance to talk to him about it."

I certainly knew how that felt. "Well, he implied that Prudence Frect might be dirty. He thinks she's the one who burned Garland Medford and my mom." I waited for Hal to yell and scream. He'd been friends with Pru for years. I fully expected him to reject the idea that she was dirty.

But he didn't. He looked thoughtful for a moment, the lines of his mouth tight and a muscle jumping in his jaw. Finally, he asked, "Do you think that was him on the phone just now?"

I thought about it, but I didn't know. "The caller was whispering. I couldn't tell who it was."

Hal stood up and started to pace, his expression tight. "From the message on the phone call, these people, whoever they are, clearly think your mother not only had the recording but that she brought it here."

"Or never took it with her when she left," I offered.

That stopped him. He glanced my way. "What are you thinking?"

I shoved my shoulders back and sighed. "I'm thinking you and I need to revisit that moldy old barn where Devon hid mom before they left Deer Hollow."

I watched as the light of understanding lit in his eyes. He nodded, a single jerk of his chin. "I'll call Arno while you get dressed."

## 13

The ramshackle barn sagged on the edge of a few hundred acres of flat farmland. Behind it, the sun rose slowly from the trees, painting the sky a gorgeous mix of pink, purple, and gold. Hal parked the Escalade at the end of the gravel drive and we climbed out. My rain boots squelched in the icy water when I stepped down.

Felly frowned at the badly weathered structure. "Seriously? Why would your mom have hidden this memory stick here?"

I stared at the barn, trying to see the half-collapsed roof and hole-riddled walls of weathered gray wood from her perspective. It was a sham. One of many the people around me had perpetrated over the last couple of years. "You'll see," I told my cousin.

Next to her, Cal shook his head. "It's never boring around you two," he told Hal and me. His brother clapped him on the shoulder. "It's not me, bro. Joey draws drama like honey draws bears."

"Appropriate metaphor," I told him. "This is a bit of a sticky wicket we've gotten ourselves into."

We headed toward the barn, water splashing icily around us. As before, nothing moved in the shadowed doorway, which had been left open since the last time we were there. As we stepped into the dusty building, a soft rustling noise announced the rapid departure of several birds. Something small, with a long, hairless tail, shot across the dirt, hay, and manure-strewn floor and disappeared through a broken board on the opposite end.

"Argghhh!" Felly said, shuddering. "Maybe I should wait in the car."

Cal tugged her close. "Scaredy cat?"

She pulled a face, then fluttered her lashes at him. "You could be my hero and carry me across the barn."

He laughed. "Fireman carry? Sure."

Since Felly, understandably, didn't want to be thrown over her boyfriend's broad shoulder like a sack of grain with her butt in the air, she stepped away from him, daring him to try with a very effective glower.

Cal laughed.

"This way," I told them and headed across the dusty space. The tack room stood open and I could see the dusty, cobwebbed remnants of a previous time. Someone had apparently had horses once, and a couple of dust-covered leather halters still hung on hooks there. Hal moved toward a plain wooden door, unobtrusive beside a couple of sagging saddle racks on the wall. The door creaked and stuck, the wood swollen with moisture. Hal managed to wrench it open and he stepped back. "Ladies first."

Felly eyed him. "You want the rats, raccoons, and bats to eat us first?"

He nodded, not a glimmer of humor on his face. "Of course. But don't worry Cal and I will rescue you before it's too late."

"Gee, thanks," she muttered, rubbing her arms over the puffy pink coat she wore.

"It's safe," I said, grinning. "I promise."

I stepped through the opening and stopped, glancing around. Despite having been there before, it still surprised me that the place was so different from the barn area. Long and narrow, the hidden room ran the length of the big building. The high windows were covered in frilly cotton curtains that let in the early morning light. Wide planks in a golden oak color covered the floor, and the walls were made of brick, painted bright white. Happy paintings depicting brightly-hued flowers and rustic country scenes turned the space into a cozy nook.

Antique brass and wood furnishing gave the room a cozy-chic feel. The queen-sized bed domi-nated one end of the room, with brightly painted tables on either side. Tall metal and wood lamps with bright white shades were perched on the bedside tables. In the center, a wooden table with two iron chairs reigned, and a multi-colored rag rug would keep diners' feet warm beneath the table. A long credenza held iron candlesticks and an array of creamy antique dishes that I could see through the leaded glass insets. The galley kitchen was bright and pleasant, with white cabinets whose doors were inlaid with leaded glass. The charcoal gray stone countertop had dramatic black veining and held a white porcelain farmhouse sink. A small stainless-steel refrigerator and stove completed the space, with a matching microwave over the stove.

A fine coating of dust covered every surface, but other than that, I imagined the room looked exactly the same as it had when my mother had lived there.

"This is awesome," Felly breathed. "I can't believe it's hidden back here."

I nodded, looking around. "The memory stick has to be here somewhere. I'll take the sleeping area."

Felly and Cal took the kitchen, and Hal searched the central area with the dining room and a small bath.

It didn't take long to find the recording.

Remembering how I'd unscrewed the finial off my four-poster brass bed when I was a kid so I could hide stuff inside, I eyed the bed and realized my mom might have remembered it too. I found what I was looking for in the third post, taped to the inside about six inches down. "Got it!" I announced.

Hal took it from me and helped me down from the mattress. Cal set the laptop he'd carried inside with him on the dining table and opened it, inserting the stick.

There was only one file on the memory stick. It was a conversation between a man and a woman. The voices were unfamiliar, but the quality of the recording wasn't clear, and I wasn't surprised I couldn't place them.

*Woman:* "It's done."

*Man:* "Target A and B are dead?"

*Woman:* "Yes."

*Man:* "And Target C?"

*Woman:* "We're still looking for C."

*Man:* "What's the problem? You told me you had a handle on it."

*Woman:* "C has proven surprisingly elusive. We'll wrap it up over the next day or so."

*Man:* "If they told him..."

"They didn't!" the woman interrupted. "I've got this. You need to trust me."

*Man:* "I hope so. The client wants us to remove an obstacle this week. If we're compromised, I want to put that on hold."

*Woman:* "We're not compromised."

*Man:* "These aren't the kind of people you want to

*cross. If we're busted, life in prison will be the upside. They'll kill us. All of us."*

When the recording ended, we were all silent for a long moment, each of us digesting what we'd heard.

Finally, I broke the silence because one question needed to be asked. "Could that be Pru?" I asked Hal. He frowned but didn't immediately respond. He stood staring down at Cal's computer.

His brother glanced up. "Pru? Do you mean Prudence Frect?"

Hal slid a look my way. "What did you think?"

"It could have been her. But the audio is kind of fuzzy. I'm sure a good electronics tech could clean it up and make a voice comparison."

My cousin lifted her perfectly-shaped light-brown brows at me.

"What?" I asked, grinning. "I watch CSI."

She chuckled.

"What about the man?" Cal asked. "Have you heard his voice before?"

I frowned. "I can't place it."

"Edward Johnston?" Hal suggested.

"Could be," I admitted. "But, since he was playing an older man, he mostly spoke with an aged timbre in his voice when I knew him. So it's hard to compare."

Johnston and his wife had lived in a very secluded

ranch on the edge of Deer County State Park. They'd done a good job of making themselves seem a decade or so older than they were the whole time I'd known them. Presumably to make themselves seem too old and feeble for anything but keeping up their spectacular ranch house in the woods. As hired killers, they'd had good reason to keep a low profile. At the time of my parents' presumed deaths, Johnston would have been in his late fifties or early sixties. Too young to have an "old man voice".

Hal's phone rang. He looked at the screen. "It's Arno."

"Hey," he said after connecting. "You're on speaker with me, Joey, Cal, and Felicity. Did you get a location on that phone?"

"I did. Pru was very helpful."

Hal slid me a look.

"You're not going to believe where the call came from," Arno told us.

"Where?"

"It's one of several phones registered to Medford Industries," Arno responded. "Surely Medford didn't return to that house. If he's trying to stay dead, it would be beyond reckless."

Somehow, I didn't figure Garland for the type to play it safe. But I was hoping his need to protect my mother would inspire him to stay away. "It's probably not him."

"Do you have an idea who called you, Joey?" Arno asked, his tone suspicious.

"No. I wish I did." Thinking of Medford's palatial home slash offices, I had a sudden thought. "Has anybody looked at Garland's right-hand man? What's his name?"

"Gil Christopher?" Cal asked. "Why do you ask?"

I shrugged. "I mean, the media are reporting that he's taking up where Garland left off. He's still living and working in Garland's mansion..."

"How is he getting away with that, anyway?" Felly asked. "He doesn't own it."

Arno's voice came through the phone. "My understanding is that, with Medford's quote unquote *death*, Christopher wrangled a controlling share of Medford Industries. Since the offices are in the building, he's taken over Medford's apartments on the top floor as his own. The stockholders voted to leave it be for now. There's no family to fight the habitation, and Christopher justifies it by claiming, truthfully, that he's working basically seven days a week, twenty hours a day."

"What does Medford Industries do anyway?" Felly asked. "I mean, the legal stuff."

"They're charity brokers," Hal said. "Medford solicits donors and manages the distribution of charity funds across the country. He also manages public relations and organizes the events that highlight donors, encouraging them to donate well and often."

"As a front for a criminal enterprise, it couldn't be better," Cal said.

"Agreed," Arno said.

"But what if Medford is working undercover for the FBI as we've been led to believe?" I asked.

"Then he's got a rat in his organization," Arno said.

"More than one rat, it sounds like," I muttered.

"Could Joey be right?" Hal asked Arno. "Could Christopher be the guy behind the smuggling etc., that Pru and the feds are investigating?"

"My understanding is that your buddy Pru looked into Christopher and cleared him. She believes our Mr. Big is someone outside Medford Industries. Someone in the government."

Cal arched a brow. "Isn't Christopher's daddy a former US Senator who's considering a run for Governor?"

Arno winced. "Yes. That had occurred to me. Frect's boss is a political animal. If he was getting political pressure from Senator Christopher, he'd be unlikely to rock that particular boat."

Hal and I shared a look. He gave me a slight nod that told me he was willing to consider his friend might be working for the wrong side. "There's something you need to know about Pru," he told Arno.

After a couple of beats of silence, Arno sighed. "Don't tell me, she's dirty?"

"It's possible," I told him. Then I told him what the pet mouse had told me in our little Interview.

"Dangit, Joey! Why didn't you tell me that?"

"We just did," I said, knowing he was right to be ticked off. "It's a serious charge, Arno. I wanted to make sure before I said anything."

"And you're sure now?"

I chewed my lip. "Um...not really." I looked at the memory stick and Hal touched my hand, shaking his head. He didn't want me to tell Arno about it. "I'm still working it through in my head. But I thought you had a right to know."

"Yeah. It would have been nice to know that before I contacted Agent Frect. I hope you're wrong about her, Joey. Because if she *is* dirty, we probably just warned her that we were looking at her partner. And we might have painted a giant target on you and your mom."

## 14

We were silent on the drive home. I was worried about my mom. The memory stick weighed heavily on me. We currently had possession of something that a lot of dangerous people were looking for. And I knew it would be wrong to give it to the wrong people just to save my mom.

But I wanted to do exactly that.

I glanced at Hal. "Why didn't you want me to tell Arno about the memory stick?"

He kept his gaze directed toward the road ahead, but I saw the muscle in his jaw tighten as it did when he was upset. "If we told him about that stick, he'd take it away from us."

"It's not cool keeping evidence from the police, bro," Cal said from the back seat.

"We'll give it to him. I just wanted some time to think about the best way to handle it. Besides, as far as we know, it's just some random recording," Hal said, glancing at his brother through the rearview mirror. "I don't know who those two people were in the recording. Do you?"

Cal looked down, shaking his head. "You're playing with fire," he said. Despite the negative message, I didn't get the impression he thought Hal was wrong.

"I'm playing with Joey's life," Hal said, a bite in his voice. "We're going to consider our options carefully before we turn this thing over."

"So, what next?" I asked.

Hal kept his gaze on the road ahead. "I need to talk to Pru."

"Do you think that's a good idea?" I asked, "If she is dirty and she finds out we have the stick..."

"Like Arno, she'll probably try to talk me into giving it to her," Hal sighed. "And then she'll destroy it."

"We could make a copy," Cal suggested.

"Yeah, we could," Hal agreed. But he frowned.

I knew what he was thinking. Pru was smart. She'd know Hal would make a copy. And she'd kill us to keep us from using it.

I hunched miserably in my seat. I'd endangered everybody I cared about. Unbidden, the caller's voice replayed itself in my mind.

*Your mother hid something there. You need to find it and bring it to me, or everyone you love is going to die.*

Unfortunately, if I did bring it to him, everybody would probably die anyway. "We need to find another way," I mumbled, not realizing I'd spoken aloud until Hal patted my knee.

"Yeah," he agreed. "We do."

---

W e stopped by the cabin so we could grab Ethel Squeaks and then headed to my house. We needed to feed the animals and ourselves and think through what we were going to do next. We agreed it was probably best if we all stayed together at my house for the foreseeable future. At least until we figured out what was going on with my mom.

I tried calling her cell phone again, but she didn't answer. Again. I disconnected and dropped my head into my hands, feeling so tired. My eyes were scratchy and my muscles felt like lead. Lack of sleep and worry were taking a toll on me.

Warm arms encircled me, and Hal's familiar scent filled my senses. I leaned my head back on his chest, sighing.

"You need to eat something."

I shook my head. "I'm not hungry."

He held me tighter, resting his chin lightly on my head.

From the kitchen came the happy sound of

playful banter and the skittering of Caphy's nails on the tile floor. The pibl and the pig were likely in full-on begging mode.

We just stood there for long moments, me with my eyes closed and Hal letting me have a few minutes where I didn't have to think.

Unfortunately, though, I never stopped thinking. My mind wouldn't quit going over all the players, looking for a way out.

He gave me one more squeeze and said, "Come on, we'll eat something and our heads will be clearer. We can come up with a plan."

I nodded, knowing he was right, and let him pull me into the kitchen.

I was forcing myself to finish a salad when my phone rang a half-hour later. I checked it and my eyes went wide. "Unknown number." I glanced at Hal. "I'm going to put it on speaker."

He nodded. The room went quiet as my friends put down their forks to listen.

"Hello?"

"Joey! Thank goodness, you're okay."

Relief loosened my tense muscles. "Mom! Where are you? I've been so worried."

"I'm sorry, honey. I'll explain everything, I promise. But I need you to come here. And you have to make sure you're not followed. It's important."

My gaze caught on Hal's. He nodded. "Where are you? Hal and I will come."

Silence met that statement. For a beat I thought she was going to fight me on bringing Hal.

Then Garland came on the line. "Remember where you saw the muddy footprint? The view is beautiful over the river. Amity can come with you. But no one else, Joey. Promise me."

"I promise. We'll be there..." I stopped, realizing if I gave a time, anyone who might be listening would know how far away our meeting spot was. It was a paranoid thought, but if we were dealing with dirty feds, bugging a phone was the least of what they might do. "—as soon as we get there," I finished lamely.

"We look forward to it." Garland disconnected without saying goodbye.

I looked at Hal. "You got that?"

Hal nodded. Our gazes held for a long moment and I knew he understood the vague reference Garland had made.

We'd recently visited a newly updated hotel on the outskirts of town that boasted a view of the river from every room. The muddy footprint had been key evidence in pinning a series of crimes on a murderer.

I didn't have to wonder how or why Garland knew about that. I'd known the hotel had recently been purchased and totally overhauled by someone from Indy with money. It didn't take much imagination to see Garland Medford as that person. It was a great investment and provided a good place for him to hide after his "death".

"Someone is probably watching your road," Cal said, carrying plates to the sink to rinse them.

Hal nodded. "You left the 4-wheeler in the back?"

Cal's gaze swung to his brother. "Yeah." He threw Hal his keys. "You can take my truck wherever you're going."

Hal grabbed the pad and pen I used for my grocery lists and jotted a name and number onto it. "Memorize this and then destroy it. If things go sideways, tell Arno where we are." He grabbed the memory stick and looked at me. I nodded in answer to the question in his eyes.

Cal's expression was tense. "You want Felly and me to draw them off?"

Hal nodded. He looked at me. "Put on warm clothes. The ride to the cabin is going to be cold."

Felly handed Cal my plate. "I'm craving ice cream."

Cal chuckled. "Ice cream! It's thirty degrees out there."

She shrugged. "I'll get hot fudge. All will be well."

"Leave it to you to turn this into an opportunity for dessert," Cal said, chuckling.

She smacked his arm. "We need to do something

while we're drawing them away. It might as well be something fun."

He waggled his brows and she smacked him again, laughing. "Toilet brain."

I left them to their playful banter and headed upstairs to layer up.

Caphy followed me, her smushy face creased with worry. When I crouched down in front of her, she gave her tail a couple of uncertain wags. "You can't come with, sweet girl. It's too dangerous. I need you to stay and protect your sisters. Okay?"

Caphy whined, her wide tongue swiping a wet path across my cheek. I wrapped my arms around her neck and gave her a hug. "I'll see you soon. I promise."

Hal appeared in the doorway. He'd layered on a flannel and a sweatshirt, topping it with his usual leather coat. He kept a bag in his car for emergencies. It apparently also contained gloves and a knit cap, which he held in one hand.

Caphy ran over and jumped up on him, putting her paws on his stomach and whining.

I laughed as I pulled on a flannel shirt and a heavy wool sweater. "She's trying to go over my head."

He scratched around her floppy ears. "You need to stay here, beauty."

She whined as if she understood the words. I sometimes wondered if she did.

I pulled heavy wool socks over my feet and grabbed a small over-the-shoulder purse, filling it with necessities before dropping it over my head.

I joined Hal in the doorway. His dark green gaze held mine for a moment, then he pulled me into a hug. "Things are going be all right, honey."

I knew he was just comforting me. We had no idea if any of it was going to be okay. But I nodded, letting myself be soothed by his words. My PI and I were a formidable team. If anybody could find a way through the current mess, we could. And our friends would back us up if it came to that.

I kissed his warm lips and sighed. "Let's go."

## 15

Cold was a gargantuan understatement. Even bundled up with several layers and a puffy coat that made me walk like a zombie because I couldn't bend my arms, I felt like a popsicle by the time Hal drove the 4-wheeler into the yard of his cabin.

He killed the lights as soon as we came out of the trees and cut the engine a moment later. "We'll leave it here," he told me, helping me off the seat. "If they're watching from the road, I don't want them to see the lights."

I let him help me unbend my frozen limbs and climb off. Then we ran toward his brother's big black truck. Hal checked his phone before we headed out of the drive.

"Cal texted us," he said. He quickly read through it, glancing my way. "They just drove by the end of my drive. There's no sign of any cars waiting here. There was one car waiting near your drive. They're following him and Felly toward Deer Hollow."

I frowned, worried for them. "What if they try to run them off the road or something?"

"Cal's one of the best drivers I know. They'll be fine. Besides, he's heading into town and will stay there until I call. We'll have Arno escort them home if Cal thinks it makes sense."

I nodded, a violent shiver overtaking me.

He started the truck, probably because he was afraid my teeth were going to fracture from clacking together. Cool air blew out of the vents. I huddled in on myself. "I might never get warm again," I told him.

Hal reached over and grabbed a gloved hand, giving it a squeeze. "It won't take long to heat up." Reversing the big truck, he turned around and headed for the road. "While we drive, let's come up with a plan. Assuming your mother and Medford are there alone, what do you think they're going to tell us?"

I shrugged. "I'm guessing Garland's trying to keep my mom safe. Maybe he wants us to help with that?"

"But she's been safe with Devon all these months. Why wouldn't she have stayed with him?"

"Maybe Dev was burned." I frowned. I hoped my mom wouldn't just leave him to fend for himself if he was in trouble. "But that would be really cold," I said aloud.

"Unless he was in more danger with her around."

I glanced at Hal, a question in my gaze.

"If he wanted to stay with her, protect her, and she knew she'd bring him down with her. Joline might have left, hoping to force him to keep his distance."

It made a twisted kind of sense. At least as much as anything else did. I sighed. "This is such a cluster."

Hal nodded.

The dark ribbon of the Fawn River glistened in the moonlight along the highway. It was too dark to see much of the land around it, but I knew the terrain that bordered the volatile river was foreboding and sharp. There were hundreds of shallow indentations worn into it from years of weather and rushing water slicing into it. I shuddered, thinking of that unruly water waiting just a few feet away from where we tore through the darkness.

Less than fifteen minutes after leaving his house, Hal pulled into The Fawn Hotel and drove slowly through the parking lot. I noted movement on the upper balcony as he pulled into the parking spot below the room we'd searched before.

He cut the engine and we eyed the window of room 210. We sat for a moment, watching for signs of habitation in the room. There was no visible light, and I wondered if that meant it was empty, or if the black-out curtains inside the room were just that good.

Hal's gaze slid along the balcony and he tensed. "He's got shooters up there."

Ice skittered through me. "Do you think it's a trap?"

He didn't respond. Like me, he probably wasn't entirely sure.

"My mom wouldn't lure us into a trap," I told him, my tone surer than I felt.

"Not voluntarily," he said, turning to stare into my eyes. Hal's expression was tight, his eyes glittering jewels in the darkness.

His implication pierced me like a knife. I sucked air as my stomach twisted. Suddenly I couldn't look at Hal. I couldn't let myself think what he was thinking. I swallowed hard. "She wouldn't let that happen," I said again. "I refuse to believe it."

He didn't respond, but the warmth of his hand squeezing my knee gave a small measure of comfort. "Let's go see what this is about," he said. No judgment. No tension. He was willing to trust me and, by extension, my mom.

I only hoped that neither of us let him down.

Hal climbed out of the truck and reached around, removing his gun from its hidey-hole in the small of his back as he came around to give me a hand down from the truck. He held the gun down by his side as we walked toward the steps that would lead us up to Room 210. His eyes continually scanned the balcony and surrounding area. When we reached the stairs, he pulled me half behind him and kept me close to his side as we slowly climbed.

Though there should have been adequate lighting at each guest door, someone must have unscrewed every other one, giving us way too many shadows to worry about.

For a moment, nothing moved in the glooms. We stopped and waited for a beat, listening. We were about to move on again when, without warning, a man walked out of the shadows beneath the next set of stairs, three rooms down.

Hal's gun hand came up. "Stop right there."

The man did as he was told, a warm chuckle emerging from the gloom. "It's good to see you again, Miss Joey. You might want to tell your man to lower the gun."

I recognized that voice. "So, how'd you get out of jail so fast?"

The pet mouse took another step and stopped, his hands raised in front of him and a crooked smile on his face. If I didn't know he was completely untrustworthy, I might have even called him charming. "I have friends in high places, don't ya know." His smile turned self-deprecating. "Now, how about you lower the gun, boyo, and I'll take ya to see the boss and his lady."

"Do you trust this guy?" Hal asked me.

I winced. That was the worst thing he could have possibly asked me. "I'm not sure."

Hal inclined his head in a single nod. "You heard the lady. She doesn't know if she can trust you. So, I'll keep my weapon. But we'll be happy to follow you to Mr. Medford and Mrs. Fulle."

The tension between the two men was more brittle than the temps. My chest hurt and I realized I wasn't breathing. I pulled air deeply into my lungs and coughed as the cold bit my throat.

When I felt like I couldn't take another minute of the standoff, A door at the far end of the building opened. A golden rectangle of light spilled out onto the balcony. A shadow showed briefly in that rectangle and then dipped as the woman who'd been standing there came outside.

I released a pent-up breath as my mother stepped onto the snow-covered boards. "Joey? Is that you? What are you doing standing out there? Come on, you'll catch your death."

Hal and I looked at pet mouse. He laughed and gave us a little bow, sweeping an arm in my mother's direction.

Joline hugged herself and stomped her feet, which, I noticed, were in fuzzy pink slippers.

Despite everything, I grinned. No matter what

was happening, my mom was going to be herself—her own, weird, wonderful self.

Without warning, tears burned my eyes.

"Aldo, have you been pestering them?" She asked pet mouse. He laughed good-naturedly, giving my mother a charming smile. "Guilty as charged, Joline."

She grinned back. "Garland asked me to tell you that we need more wine."

"Yes, ma'am." Mouse winked at me as we moved quickly past him. "Relegated to doing liquor runs." He shook his head. "It's a travesty."

I found myself grinning. It wouldn't hurt the cocky son of a gun to be knocked down a few pegs.

I hurried into my mom's arms, giving her a slightly desperate hug. "I'm so glad you're okay," I whispered.

She laughed and rubbed my back. "Of course I'm okay. Why wouldn't I be?" She tugged me toward the door. "It's freezing out here. Let's have something hot and we can talk."

I expected a hotel room, with a bed, a small table, a couple of nightstands, a closet and a small bathroom like Room 210.

When I walked through the unnumbered door on the opposite end of the building from 210, it was like walking into one of those magic tents in a fantasy story, where the space inside didn't seem to match the space promised on the exterior.

The room was huge, with high ceilings, hard-wood floors, and a wall of windows along the back, overlooking the river. A large rug in a dark mauve color anchored the light wood floor. Expensive cream leather furniture was arranged around the rug, facing one of those artsy gas fireplaces that hung on the wall. The only windows ranged along the back, overlooking the dark, glossy surface of the Fawn. The entry door closed behind us with a solid sound that told me it was heavier than the usual hotel door.

The walls were painted a soft, creamy white. I smiled when I saw the paintings on the walls. They were similar to the natural art my mom had favored in her barn hideaway. Similar enough to make me realize Garland had been inside that hidey-hole. In fact, the entire room fit my mother's tastes perfectly. As if it had been decorated with her in mind.

"Come on, Garland's downstairs."

I felt my eyes go wide. "Downstairs?"

She laughed gaily. "It's a bit of a shock, isn't it. When Garland bought this place to rehab and update, he'd intended this apartment to be his little hideaway when he needed to get out of the city. He's always loved the raw energy and power of the Fawn. And when he was attacked..." She frowned. "Well, it's worked out well." She motioned toward a stair-case at the side of the room. It was one of those circular jobs that looked good but which everybody hates.

The wood was blond to match the wood flooring of the elegant main room. Behind the floating staircase were double wood doors that opened up into a large bedroom suite.

Voices rose up through the open space around the staircase.

Garland wasn't down there alone.

I glanced at Hal as we descended behind my mom. He'd put his gun away, but there was tension along his jaw that told me he didn't really trust what we were walking into.

The room we stepped down into mapped to the one above in size and shape. A kitchen with marble counters, stainless steel appliances, and white cabinets stretched along one end, covering all but the space of a sliding glass door. Men with guns moved through the yard beyond the door. They shifted in and out of shadow, mainly invisible unless you were looking for them.

Garland was standing in front of a fireplace, the flames crackling merrily behind him and the faint smell of woodsmoke testifying to the fact that it was a real fire. He held a crystal tumbler with about two fingers worth of amber liquid. His expression, when he turned to us, was relaxed. "Ah, here they are now." He jerked his chin in our direction, and his visitor stood from the spot on the long, russet couch where he'd been sitting.

When the second man turned around and gave me a careful smile, I gasped in surprise.

"Hello, Joey. Hal."

Uncle Devin stood there with a drink, looking for all the world like he'd always belonged.

## 16

"Surprised to see me?" Dev asked.

My mother went to stand next to Garland. He wrapped an arm around her waist and kissed her temple, chuckling as she took his glass away from him and sipped. She tried to give it back, but he shook his head. "I'll get another. Hal, Joey, would you like a drink?"

"No," Hal said gruffly. Then he seemed to realize how antagonistic he'd sounded and said, "But thanks."

"Coffee?" I asked.

Garland headed into the kitchen and grabbed a mug, filling it from a steaming pot. "Sit. Catch up. I understand Devon came to you looking for us. I apologize that we've put you in the middle of things again. I assure you..." He handed me a steaming mug of coffee. "Your mother and I never intended for that to happen."

I sipped the coffee because I didn't know what else to do. My mind was whirling with a feeling of having stepped into Wonderland. Nothing was the way I thought it should have been.

Garland poured himself another drink and rejoined my mother in front of the fire. He slid his gaze over Hal and me, still standing, and one eyebrow arched. "I can tell you're not interested in small talk."

"No," I agreed. "I'm not. You three have kept me in the dark for almost three years. Clearly, everything I believed was a lie. It's past time you told me what's really going on here." I fixed a glare on my mother. "You owe me that."

She blanched, her gaze falling away. "You're right, sweetie. We do owe you an explanation. But I'm not sure it's wise for you to know everything."

I stiffened as I realized that, after everything she'd put me through...after leaving me alone all those months, feeling alone and scared...she still didn't want to tell me. I walked to the kitchen and slammed the mug down on the counter. "Let's go, Hal."

"Joey, please?"

I spun around, so angry I was shaking. "Please? Please what, mother? Please keep being a patsy.

Please don't rock the boat and make things uncomfortable? Please just suck all the lies down and go on as if none of this ever happened?" I shook my head. "I will do that," I told her, earning myself a surprised look from the guilty trio in front of me. "But you are all dead to me. I don't want to see you again. I don't want to hear from you. I will do my best not to care what happens to you. I'm done being the clueless patsy whose life you keep dropping into when it's useful."

I headed for the stairs. Hal fell in beside me, his hand warm and supportive on my back.

"No, Joey, don't leave," Devon said. He took several long strides to catch up and then jolted to a stop when Hal turned to him, his hand on the gun at his back. "Stay back, Little," he growled.

I lifted my foot to the first step and was jolted to a stop by the soft, anguished sound of my mother's voice. "Joey?" I stilled, my gaze on the steps ahead. I was afraid if I looked at my mother, I'd give in, or worse...I'd start to cry.

"You're right. We've been unfair."

I finally turned to her.

Joline looked up at Garland. He touched her jaw with a tender finger, nodding. "Tell her."

Something inside me unwound at those words. Suddenly, I was able to pull air into my lungs again.

Finally.

I'd finally find out why my world had been turned upside down.

I returned to the living room and sat down, perched on the edge of the couch. Hal stood behind me, a reassuring presence at my back.

"Where should I start?" my mother asked no one in particular.

"Start at the beginning," I said. "Tell me everything."

Joline set her drink down on the mantle and joined me on the couch. She half-turned, clasping my hands in an icy grip. She gave me a sad smile, squeezing my fingers. "Your dad and I were involved in things you didn't know about."

I stiffened, suddenly certain I was going to hate what she said next.

She noticed. "It's not like that, sweetie. We didn't do anything illegal. We helped the FBI and Garland move people and things that bad people wanted."

"Like Sasha?" I asked.

Joline nodded. "Yes."

"Who was she, really?" I asked. She looked to Garland for help.

"A friend," he responded, looking sad. "And a business associate. Sasha worked with Prudence Frect, as did I."

Hal stirred behind me. "Pru isn't dirty?"

Garland frowned. "No. And neither am I."

I stared at him. "Every source everywhere would

disagree with that. According to the media and law enforcement, you're involved in everything from drugs to human slavery."

He inclined his head. "Some of that is speculation and rumor. We allowed it to stand because it helped me retain my cover. But the truth is, I went to Pru when I realized my business partner was involved in things that weren't legal. With people who weren't reputable." He frowned. "I've been in place for five years, watching, waiting, recording. That night..." He glanced at my mother. "Joline and your father were doing me a favor by helping Sasha. But something went wrong. Someone found out Sasha was transporting key evidence that had the potential to take down someone powerful." He frowned at Devon. "Someone got to them before we could intervene."

I looked at Devon too. He was standing near the window, staring into the darkness with a drink clutched, forgotten in his hand. He must have seen Garland's reflection in the glass. He must have known the man was looking his way. But he didn't turn.

"Was it Devon?" I asked. "Did he double-cross you?"

Joline gasped. "No. Oh my goodness, no. Dev wouldn't do that."

In the reflection of the glass, I thought I saw my

godfather grimace. He lifted the tumbler in his hand and drank, but he didn't respond.

Seeing that grimace, I wasn't so sure. "Uncle Dev, don't you have something to say?"

He sighed but remained standing as he was. "I loved your father," he said, his voice husky with emotion. "We were inseparable as kids. As adults, we were as close as brothers. Even when he got married, I stayed with him as a pseudo partner at the auction." He smiled then, a taut curve of his lips that had no humor in it. "I was just an employee, but he treated me like a partner."

"He considered you an equal," my mother said gently. "He loved you too."

Devon nodded, taking another drink, his movements stiff and angry. "But I couldn't save him that night. I tried. God knows I tried. But I was too late. When I saw the fireball..." His throat worked and he looked down, struggling with his emotions. It was a moment before he could go on. "At first, I thought you'd died too," he told my mother. She knew he was speaking to her, and she gave a shaky sigh, her eyes glassy with tears. "I was so relieved when I realized it wasn't you." He turned then, his expression filled with rage.

The rage caught me off guard. I'd expected sadness. Regret.

"I saved you," he told her. "I dragged you kicking and screaming from that burning wreckage and hid you, protected you. But you never trusted me, did you? You never did."

Tears slid down her cheeks. She fixed a look on him that was more apology than regret. "Someone gave Belle and Edward Johnston the information that they were going to be landing at that time." Her mouth tightened with her own anger. "You told Brent to come back. You were the reason my husband was there."

She stopped short of accusing him of being the reason they'd died, but it hung between them anyway...stark and horrible.

"Don't you think I've carried that with me since then, Joline? Don't you believe it weighs me down every day? I was only trying to save him. To protect him."

"Who gave you the information that the flight was compromised?" Hal asked.

My mother jerked in surprise at the sound of his voice. As if she'd forgotten he was there.

When Devon didn't respond, Garland spoke up. "I did," he said, shocking us all. "Through Pru."

The look on my mother's face told me she hadn't known. "I'm sorry, Jo. I wasn't at liberty to talk with you about my arrangement with the FBI. The fewer people who knew, the better."

"Wait," I said, frowning. "Devon, you worked for Pru too?"

Rather than answering directly, he said. "I'll bet you never knew I'd been a cop, did you?"

My eyes went wide. "Seriously? When? Were you ten years old at the time?"

He chuckled, scrubbing his face and the tears I hadn't realized he'd shed. "The Feds were at a job fair my senior year. I thought it would be cool, and I interviewed to be an analyst when I graduated. But they didn't need another analyst in Indianapolis. They wanted me to train as a cop and work under-cover for them." He laughed harshly. "I thought I was James Bond. I was insufferable. It's a wonder my fellow rookies didn't shoot me in a back alley."

"Needless to say, being a cop didn't scratch the itch that first exposure to the FBI created. I was young and stupid. I washed out. I came back here and helped your dad start the auction. Your mom was pregnant with you the first time the feds asked me to go undercover for them. I jumped at the chance, even knowing it was a short assignment that required me to stay employed at the auction. Brent knew about the assignments. He supported them, even letting me take the truck into Indy when I needed a reason to be there. Eventually, I got a call from Prudence Frect. She asked me to keep an eye on the pretty teenaged daughter of a wealthy Arab diplomat who'd reneged on his payment for an illegal delivery of stolen artwork to Dubai. Pru had heard rumors that the girl was going to be kidnapped as leverage. She wanted somebody who didn't look like a cop to keep an eye on her. So I took the auction truck and Pru got me access to a house across the street from the target. It was good cover. I spent weeks inside that house, watching the girl."

"What happened?" I asked, pulled into the story despite myself.

"They made their play one night in the target's driveway, grabbing her when she stumbled out of her car after a night of partying. I notified Pru and managed to block the drive with the auction truck until she could get there."

My mom grimaced. "Brent was so ticked about the giant dent in the truck."

Devon chuckled. "He was. Until the feds offered him twice what the stupid truck was worth as recompense."

Mom nodded. "True."

"Anyway, long story short, we saved the girl. But her parents were both killed that night. The would-be kidnappers were killed too." He looked at Garland. "But we traced one of them back to Medford Industries."

Garland nodded. "I'd suspected Gil of being behind some kidnappings of prominent people for a while. His Dubai connections were troublesome. Young American women are prized there." He grimaced with distaste. "When Pru came to me and all but confirmed it, Sasha and I decided to go for a sting. She got lucky months later, catching what we believe was Gil and some unknown woman on a phone call where they seemed to be discussing the murders and attempted kidnapping that Devon had witnessed."

I glanced at my mother, and she stared back, her expression blank. At that moment, I realized she hadn't told Devon about the memory stick.

"You didn't trust me with that recording, did you, Joline?" Devon growled out.

Mom and I swung our gazes his way, shocked at the anger in his voice.

"I gave you dozens of opportunities to tell me where it was. But you never did."

Joline shook her head. "I don't know…"

"Save it!" Devon barked. "You found it that night near the wreckage. I put it together later and realized you had to have. You were holding something back from me the whole time. Something that could have given me chops with the FBI. Something that could have taken a very bad man down." He glared at her. "Why, Joline? Why would you hide that stick? Why wouldn't you turn it over? Unless you were the woman on that tape."

I gasped, enraged. Hal placed a hand on my shoulder. "That's ridiculous!" I said, jumping to my feet.

Amazingly, my mom didn't defend herself. She

just sat there, staring at Devon with a hurt expression on her face.

Then I looked at Garland and saw the pain there, and I knew. She hadn't given the FBI that memory stick because she'd been afraid it was Garland in the recording.

How horrible it must have been for them both to have that between them. Garland shook his head and looked away. His pain showed in every line of his long, elegant form.

An odd popping sounded beyond the glass doors. Light bloomed in a flower pattern in the night.

Hal grabbed my arm. "Joey, we need to go."

Devon ran toward the couch. I wasn't sure if he was going to attack us or help us.

I would never find out.

The sliding door shattered and we dove toward the ground, scrabbling behind the furniture.

Footsteps pounded overhead.

Covering me with his body, Hal hurried me toward the stairs. Garland grabbed my mom and followed.

That was when I realized Devon wasn't coming. I turned to find him sprawled across the carpet, his back glistening with blood and glass. "Uncle Dev!"

Hal tugged me. "Come on. We'll send help back for him. But we need to get out now. Before our options are cut off."

I let him pull me up the stairs, and we started to run. We didn't get far. Garland and my mom weren't moving. And I soon realized why.

Edward Johnston was standing between us and the door. And he was holding a deadly looking shotgun on us. "Surprise!" he said with a grin. "It looks like we're going to get to play, after all."

## 17

I gasped in shock. Johnston's brows lifted, a mean smile stretching across his lean face. Even with the short-cropped beard and dyed black hair, I recognized the craggy features of Edward Johnston. "Miss Fulle. It's nice to see you again," he purred. Then he slid a hungry glance over Joline. "And your mother too."

Garland moved between Johnston and Joline, his fists clenched. "You touch her and you'll die."

The sound of bullets being chambered lifted the tension in the room by several degrees.

Garland stilled. "How many of my people did you kill?" he ground out.

Johnston shrugged. "Not many. Not so far. But you can be the first if you try my patience."

"What do you want?" my mom asked. She still seemed more ticked off than scared. I stared at her in awed surprise. Who was that woman? I hadn't known my mother at all.

"You know what I want, Sweet Joline." He swung the shotgun my way. "And you're going to give it to me, or your beautiful daughter will die."

Hal moved then, a fast, deadly threat. Before Johnston knew what had hit him, Hal's hand was on the shotgun and his other hand was heading for the older man's smug face.

The shotgun went off, the concussive force painful and debilitating by its nearness. I hunched over with a small cry and felt Johnston brush past. Before I could wrap my head around what he was doing, he'd pistol-whipped Hal on the side of the head.

I screamed as Hal went down, blood spreading from a nasty gash at his hairline.

I fought to get to him but couldn't. Hard, ruthless hands grabbed me and, without any further discussion, I found myself thrown over somebody's shoulder and hauled out of the apartment in a fireman's carry. I fought my captor until he placed a gun at my temple. Then, I stilled.

But I threw a look behind us as I was carried through the door.

And saw both Garland and Hal lying on the floor, bleeding.

My screams were desperate and filled with fear. And they were met only with more screaming.

To my horror, I realized they'd grabbed my mother too.

———

They'd put hoods over our heads and flung us into the back of some kind of van. The only thing I'd seen during the long drive to wherever they'd taken us were headlights flashing past. I couldn't hear much. My ears still rang from the shotgun blast. The rough grumble of male voices and the bump of tires on asphalt were the only sensory clues I could gather, except for a sour stench that I was pretty sure was dirty socks. The carpet beneath us was slightly gritty too, as if covered with sand or small gravel.

It was clearly a work van of some kind. But I didn't smell gardening supplies or paint, so I eliminated those as possibilities.

My mother didn't stir for the entire trip, which I thought was about an hour. And when the flash of passing headlights became more frequent, I guessed we were close to Indianapolis.

The van slowed, reducing the road noise.

"...do with them?" an unfamiliar voice asked.

I realized I was getting my hearing back and strained to hear the conversation.

"...up to him."

"...kill..."

Ice clawed along my spine. I didn't need to hear the rest of that sentence to know the men were talking about killing us.

Johnston was a bloodthirsty jerk. I couldn't believe I'd let him pet my dog.

Beside me, Joline moaned softly.

I did a worm crawl trying to get closer to her...no easy task with my wrists and ankles bound. "Mom?" I whispered when I'd gotten as close as my restraints and her fetal position would allow. "Are you okay?"

She groaned again. "Head's killing me."

I winced. I was pretty sure they'd hit her. She'd been screaming and fighting them with everything she had. She'd made me proud. "It's going to be okay," I told her, though I wasn't sure I believed that myself. "Hal and Garland will come for us."

She didn't respond. I wasn't sure if that was because she didn't believe me or because she was in too much pain.

The van stopped finally, and I stilled, listening to the front doors open and slam shut.

I leaned close to mom. "They're coming for us, mom. We need to fight them. Can you do that?"

Nothing. She must have passed out again.

Dangit!

I couldn't fight my way out of whatever we'd gotten ourselves into without her. I'd have to wait. Bide my time. Until she was able to fight with me.

*And if she isn't ever ready to fight?* my traitorous brain asked. Then...I didn't know.

The doors wrenched open with a squeal. Rough hands grabbed at my ankles. "Home sweet home," Johnston's cold voice said as he pulled on my legs. Fire burned across my exposed skin from being dragged over the musty carpet. Making a sudden decision, I bit back a cry at the pain and forced myself to go limp.

I'd play dead until I saw an opening. And then... well...then I'd hope we got a chance to make a move. Because I really didn't like our chances if we didn't find a way out of there.

---

We were thrown into a room, our wrists and ankles still bound and the hoods still covering our heads. The carpet beneath me was plusher than the carpet inside the van had been. It also smelled a lot better. But I could tell by the lack of light and shadow playing over the hood that we were in darkness.

The room smelled slightly musty, as if it hadn't been used for a while. Aside from the occasional distant sound of a closing door, I heard nothing that suggested there were even people in the place where they'd put us.

Could we get that lucky? Maybe they'd thrown

us into a guest house or something and hadn't left a guard to watch us. It seemed unlikely, but I was pretty sure Johnston would underestimate us. To his way of thinking, we were just two women who'd never had to physically fight to save ourselves. Bound and without weapons. I'd probably underestimate us too.

My mother would be safe until they had the memory stick. And we couldn't tell them where it was even if we wanted to, because neither of us knew where it was.

Cal and Felly had taken it with them when they'd gone into town for ice cream. They'd likely have given it to Arno, by now, which meant it was already too late for the people who were holding us hostage.

As soon as they realized they wouldn't be getting the memory stick from us, we were no longer useful.

So I couldn't let them realize that.

I had to stall.

And I had to pray Hal and Garland managed to find us before Johnston and his gang decided we weren't worth the trouble of keeping around.

I struggled against the zip ties binding my wrists until my wrists were bloody and my ankles ached. I managed to loosen the binding on my ankles. But not enough to get my feet free. Panting, sweaty, and in pain, I finally subsided, deciding to take a short break before trying again.

Sometime later, I jerked awake from a dream where I was drowning, my chest screaming and my heart pounding painfully against my ribs. I rolled to my back and used my stomach muscles to sit up, spitting the hood out of my mouth where I'd breathed it in.

I sucked in a careful breath, and precious air filled my lungs. I sat there in a full-out panic, my heart pounding a terrified staccato from the residue of the dream.

"Joey?" My mom's voice cracked on my name, and she coughed. I could hear her moving around on the carpet, her silk blouse swishing noisily. "Where are we?"

"I don't know. They drove for about an hour, I think, so I'm guessing Indy."

There was more swishing, followed by a soft grunt. My mom's shoulder bumped mine. "How big is this place? Could you tell?"

"Pretty big, I think. It took them a good fifteen minutes' walk to get here from the van."

She sighed, and something heavy landed on my shoulder. I smelled the fresh lilac scent of her hair. "I'm sorry, sweetie. This is all my fault."

"No. It's freaking Edward Johnston's fault. It's not our fault we were kidnapped."

She didn't respond.

I remembered she'd been knocked out. "How's your head?"

"Killing me." She lifted her head and I could feel her wriggling against me. "What kind of bindings are these? They're hard, but they don't feel like metal."

"Zip ties, I think. I've been working mine, and I think they're looser." I didn't feel bad about stretching the truth to make her feel better. I'd get the stupid things off if it killed me.

A distant voice jerked our attention away from the bindings.

Mom huddled closer. "Somebody's coming."

"I don't recognize the voice, do you?"

There was a beat of silence. "Mom?"

The lock turned in the door and light slanted across my hood. I could see a tall, well-made form backlit a few feet away. The man didn't say anything for a moment. Then he moved into the room and bent over my mom. I struggled to get to him, swinging my bound legs in his direction and missing.

He tugged her hood off and silence pulsed through the room.

Finally, he said. "Joline. Why didn't you just give me the stick? It would have made all this so much easier."

Shock flared through me. They knew each other?

"Let Joey go," my mom said. "She has nothing to do with this."

"And you do?" The words shot out of my mouth before I could stop them. "Mom, what in the world have you gotten yourself into?"

The man reached down and pulled mom to her feet. I couldn't see well enough through the weave of the hood to see what he did with her, but I heard the soft compression of a mattress. "I'm sorry you had to go through this," his voice was gentle, almost tender. Was he acting?

A moment later, I felt his hands on me. I lost my mind, thrashing against his touch.

He released me and whistled. A beat later, I heard the sound of footsteps in the hallway outside and another man came into the room. "Yes, sir?"

"Put Miss Fulle in that chair, please."

I struggled against the painful hold of the second man, but he was much bigger and stronger and easily maneuvered me to an upholstered chair. He yanked off the hood.

"Thanks, Jack. Can you flip the lights on and then close the door. But stay close in case I need something."

"Yes, sir."

The lights seemed way too bright. My eyes watered, and I squinted against the sudden glare.

As soon as I could keep my eyes open, I searched for my mom. She was sitting on the edge of a queen-sized bed, still bound, and her eyes were shadowed with purple arcs that told me better than anything how much her head was hurting her.

I jerked an angry glare toward the man. "They hit her on the head. She's in pain. Give her something." I barely recognized the snarl that passed for my own voice.

The man gave me a condescending smile. "You'll want to check some of that attitude, Miss Fulle. You don't exactly have bargaining power right now."

I jerked my gaze toward my mom. "Who is this douche nozzle?"

She barked out a laugh, which made me feel better. "Joey, meet Gil Christopher. Garland's partner in Medford Industries."

The man chuckled softly. "I guess you haven't heard, beautiful Joline. I'm nobody's partner now. Our dear Garland was kind enough to leave me controlling interest in the company when he died. Such a loss," he said, feigning sadness. "He'll be missed."

"Yeah, there's just one little problem," I snarled at the man. "Garland's not dead. And he's not going to be happy about what you did to my mom."

"Oh, but he is dead, pretty Joey. I'll admit it took us a couple of tries, but second time's a charm." He chuckled.

Mom gasped, her eyes filling with tears. "You're going to be sorry."

Christopher shrugged. "That's possible. But not

likely." He ran a finger over my mother's jaw. She jerked her head away from his touch. "Now, if you don't want your beautiful daughter to join Garland in the grave, you'll want to tell me where that memory stick is."

"Why do you want it so badly?" I asked. I was relieved to see him turn away from my mother and focus on me. I needed to buy us some time. And it was going to be trickier than I thought. If Garland was really dead... Pain stabbed me in the chest. If Garland was gone, could Hal...? No. I wouldn't go there. He had to be okay. "Are you afraid the police will recognize your voice?" I asked Christopher.

Because it *had* been his voice on the recording. I'd bet my life on it. I actually *was* betting my life on it. Both mine and my mother's.

## 18

Something ugly happened to Christopher's face. Something feral. "Have a care, Joey Fulle. I have no compunction about killing you. The only thing keeping you alive right now is that memory stick. If you don't have it..." He shrugged and, like magic, a small, silver gun appeared in his hand. The muzzle was suddenly pressed against Joline's temple.

To her credit, she didn't respond, except to close her eyes. Only the taut lines of her slender frame told me she was scared out of her mind. But she didn't want me to know it. When she opened her eyes again, they were fairly glowing with rage. "You can kill me, Christopher. Twice," she smiled to let him know that was a dig about failing to get Garland the first time. "But it won't bring you that memory stick. I don't have it. I don't know what you're talking about."

Wow. She was good. I almost believed her.

He chuckled, his posture relaxed. "Is that so? That's strange because clearly your daughter has heard the recording." He turned to me, his expression hard with rage. "Haven't you, Joey?"

I fought to keep shock and fear off my face, but I was pretty sure he saw it in my eyes. My heart pounded against my ribs, and I saw stars as panic coated me like a stain. I'd screwed up. In wanting to taunt him, I'd let him know I'd listened to the recording. Dangit! I was so stupid!

My mother's face was chalky with fear. But her fear wasn't for herself. It was for me. "Give it to him, sweetie. It's not worth dying over."

I swallowed hard, my gaze locked on his. "Yeah, there's only one problem. He can't let me live. I heard his voice on that tape."

I could hardly breathe as the panic made the room spin around me. I was going to die.

"Who else listened to the recording, Joey, hm?" He laughed when I flinched. "Ah, yes. I see I have many loose ends to tidy up."

What the heck. If I was going to die, maybe I could at least save Hal and Cal and...my throat closed with horror...Felly.

No! She couldn't be dragged into it.

Steeling my resolve, I straightened my back and said, "It's too late, Christopher. Prudence Frect already has the stick. It's over. You've lost."

For a long moment, I didn't think he'd heard. Then a fine tremor slid through him, making its way up his large frame to the hand still clutching the gun.

In that moment, I was certain he was going to kill my mom.

I suddenly found it hard to breathe. The coward in me wanted to close my eyes, but I forced myself to hold his gaze.

The tremor in Christopher's tan, muscular arm increased, and the muscles of his forearm bulged as if he were squeezing the gun hard. Or the trigger.

I forced a terrified breath into my lungs. "You should probably get out of here before the FBI comes," I said. My voice was breathy, with a slight tremble in it, but I managed to hold his gaze. "They know we're here."

A quick double staccato knock burst the silence. I jumped, my eyes swinging to my mom's. Tears were sliding down her cheeks, and it almost broke me. My eyes stung with answering tears.

"Come!" Christopher barked out.

The door opened, and the gunman who'd stuffed me into the chair stuck his head inside. "Sir, there's something you need to see."

With a glare that promised horrible things to come, Christopher turned away from me and pocketed the gun. Without another word, he followed the man out of the room and closed the door behind him.

I looked at my mom. "We don't have much time." I stood and looked down at my ankles, they were too tightly bound to allow any kind of walking, so I hopped, feeling like an idiot. When I got to the bed, I dropped down onto my knees and turned around. "Get on the floor next to me," I told my mom. To her credit, she did as I asked without argument.

"What's the plan?" she asked, squirming around to face away from the bed like me.

"Can you grab the mattress? We need to push it over as far as we can."

Nodding, Joline spread her palms as far as the zip ties would allow and we pushed. It barely moved. We didn't have much leverage from the floor. "Maybe if we stood up," I said.

Grunting and panting, we pressed against the mattress with our backs and used it to stand, then we tried pushing again.

After a few determined shoves, it moved a few inches. By the time I heard the familiar pop of gunfire outside the walls, we'd moved it over a good ten inches. The box spring was easier to move because of its firmer frame. We ended up sitting down and shoving it over with our feet, which would have been a better way to move the mattress too.

Oh well. Lesson learned. The next time I was

kidnapped, bound at wrist and ankle with zip ties, and needed to move a mattress, I'd be more efficient.

"Now what?" mom asked.

"Now we use the sharp metal edge of this bed frame..."

"To break the ties," she finished for me. Her expression lit with understanding. "Smart girl. I knew you took after me."

I laughed wetly, tears sliding down my cheeks for no apparent reason. "Do your ankles first. That way, if we have to move before we get completely free, we'll have mobility."

We set to work and made quick work of our ankle bindings.

I'd just broken my wrist binding when I heard footsteps pounding our way. "We're out of time," I looked at Joline's wrists. Blood coated the fair skin around the tie and slicked the binding. She was struggling.

Jumping to my feet, I grabbed her under the arms and wrenched her off the floor with more strength than I should have had. She gave a surprised little gasp as her feet left the floor. I grabbed her arm and pulled her toward the door. The footsteps stopped on the other side of the door, and I heard heavy breathing.

I reached up and flicked off the light. At that point, I'd take any advantage I could find.

I pressed my mom against the wall and looked

around for something I could use to fight them off. I spotted a metal horse sculpture on a table four feet away.

I dove toward the statue just as the door started to open. Squeezing it hard in a shaky right hand, I tried not to think about the intelligence of going after a guy with a gun when I was armed only with a solid and admittedly heavy chunk of metal.

The gunman seemed to sense that we were waiting for him. He only opened the door a few inches and led with his gun, probably thinking that would be a deterrent.

Bad decision on his part.

As his hand cleared the door, Joline threw her weight into the heavy wood, and it slammed into the guy's wrist.

He grunted in pain and the door slammed back, hitting my mom hard enough to send her to the floor.

Johnstone stood in front of the door, slowly reaching over to flick the light on. His smile made my stomach twist, nausea blooming. "Nobody here to save you now, Joey Fulle. I've been looking forward to this for a long time."

I screamed and ran at Johnston, the statue lifted above my head. I'd intended to go for his gun hand, but, at the last moment, I changed my mind. As the assassin swung around, gun up and pointed between my eyes, I threw the statue, aiming for his head.

As soon as the metal left my hand, I dropped to the floor like a rock. The bullet sheared past me, too close, leaving behind the stench of burnt hair as it struck an antique dresser with a mirror. The impact shattered the glass into a thousand shards and pieces.

Johnston staggered under the impact of the heavy statue but somehow kept his feet. I shoved off the floor and hit him in the middle, sending us both to the ground in a painful and ungainly heap.

The gouge I'd made in his forehead with the statue was bleeding copiously, blinding him. I used that to my advantage, slamming the heel of my hand into his nose.

Unfortunately, the blow didn't land hard enough to do any damage. My hand slid in the blood, muting the effect of my punch.

Johnston swung a fist, slamming it into my side. Agony flared through me, robbing me of the ability to breathe. Wheezing painfully, I tried to knee him in the family vault, but he blocked me with his thigh and swung at me again.

I scrambled away, catching my foot in the carpet in my hurry to escape.

With an enraged growl, Johnston shoved to his feet and moved over me. Mopping blood from his eyes with his shirt sleeve, he lifted the gun, clearly intending to pistol whip me with it.

He never got the chance.

A slender frame with dark, murderous eyes rose up behind him and slashed toward his back with a large shard of mirror glass. The shard slipped into his flesh with a wet thwucking sound. I grimaced as he fell.

Snatching my feet away from the spot where the assassin landed, I scrambled away, eyeing him for signs that he was getting back up.

Johnston wasn't going anywhere. He'd landed flat on his face without trying to shield himself, a grisly slice of glass resting between his shoulder blades.

Joline walked over and offered me her hand. "Ready?"

I couldn't help it, I barked out a slightly hysterical laugh. "Yeah. Let's get out of here."

Fortunately for us, Christopher and his guys were too busy fending off the array of local cops and FBI to notice a couple of exhausted, bloody women searching for an exit out of the enormous office complex. We quickly realized we were on the topmost level, probably the residence floor of Garland's mansion.

We found a stairwell and ran down the stairs until we hit the first level.

By the time we slid through an emergency exit in the lower level offices, Pru was walking Gil Christopher toward an FBI vehicle parked crossways on the long, paved drive, lights flaring into the night.

We stood in the relative silence for a beat, taking in the array of flashing lights and uniforms. The lines of once-armed men kneeling in the grass with guns pointed at them.

"It's over?" Joline whispered, sounding like she didn't quite believe it. I wrapped an arm around her shoulders and rested my head against hers. "It's over." I took a deep breath of the clean, cool night air and just stood there for a moment longer, working up the energy to face the police with their guns, questions, and instant suspicions.

Joline moved from foot to foot and I looked down, seeing only one fuzzy pink slipper on her feet. She gave me an embarrassed smile. "They were my favorite."

"We'll get you another pair." I hugged her against my side. "Maybe I'll get a pair too."

She laughed.

Then I thought of Hal and my stomach twisted. I wasn't sure I wanted to know if he was gone. Ignorance allowed me to breathe. It allowed me to believe that we'd have a future together. It let me bask in the idea that my fur babies still had a furless daddy.

Tears slipped from my eyes. Joline looked at me and pulled me in for a hug. Her cheeks were wet too. I suddenly felt guilty for my pain, when I knew hers had to be worse. She'd loved and lost my dad. And now she'd loved and lost another man.

Life sucked.

"Well now, isn't that sweet?"

We jumped and spun around to find Aldo holding a short, deadly-looking shotgun on us.

His smile was feral. "Looks like I have a little leverage now, don't I?"

I tried to step in front of my mom, but she grabbed my hand and held me back.

"Leverage for what?" Joline asked, tugging me behind her.

"I think you know the answer to that, Mrs. Fulle."

"I don't have the memory stick," she told him. "I never did. I heard the police have it."

The distant flash of police lights danced across his face, giving him a sickly hue. "Do they? Well, then, you're going to have to think of some way to get it back from them, aren't you?"

"We can't do that," I told him. "They've already got a case against your boss." I frowned, seeing the look of pure rage flash across his handsome face. Recognition sparked in my brain, shocking me to my core. I quickly assessed his age to be close to mine and slid a look over the longish, curly dark hair. His charcoal eyes were rimmed in thick mahogany lashes. His build was tall and lean. Suddenly, I knew who Aldo was. "Why would you turn against your dad?"

Joline sucked in a quiet gasp, her muscles going taut beneath my fingers.

Aldo's lips tightened. "Prudence Frect thought she was being so clever. She had spies everywhere inside his organization. She liked to double and triple her options. It would have been a smart play, except for the fact that it left too many open switches. At any given time, she had several areas of possible weakness. And when she recruited me, she opened herself up to a whole mess of problems." He chuckled, clearly enjoying himself. "I worked both sides against the middle. Kept everyone's balls in the air. Divvied up information. It's been fun and challenging." He laughed with clear enjoyment. "And in the end, I had the sure knowledge of seeing him get taken down. Of seeing him suffer." The smile turned into something much less pleasant. "Like I suffered because of him."

"But, I don't understand," Joline said. "From what I've seen, he's always been kind to you."

"Has he?" The words fired from Aldo's lips like bullets and smacked into my mom, making her flinch. "Or was I just an inconvenient detail he needed to keep neutralized, so I didn't cause more trouble for him?"

"To be fair," Joline told the younger man. "He didn't know about you for a long time."

Aldo sneered. "He doesn't care about me. He doesn't even really believe he's my father. To him, I'm just a favor for a friend. Nothing more." His expression darkened with rage. "Well, that 'friend' killed your husband, didn't she? She will ultimately be the cause of both of your deaths too." His smile was mean. "I'll make sure he knows that before he dies."

My head was spinning. Just how many layers were there to my mom's cache of secrets? I needed to know what Aldo was talking about, but judging by the rage the subject was causing him, I needed to distract him more. "Why do you want that memory stick?" I asked Aldo. "What good will it do you?"

"So much good," he said. "If it's destroyed."

At that moment, I finally understood. "You want Garland to be blamed for everything, don't you? You want Gil Christopher's crimes to fall into Garland's lap, freeing Christopher and sending Garland to prison."

"Public opinion is already against him," Aldo said with obvious satisfaction. "Law enforcement believes he's guilty of everything that's been rumored to have happened through Medford Industries. After all, the company bears his name. He's ultimately responsible. And the evidence will all go against him. He won't have a chance. As soon as that stick is destroyed, we'll start leaking all the damning information we have stockpiled. Gil has promised me big things. We'll be partners. But in order for that to happen, my father either needs to die or go to prison. Then we'll have a clean slate. And together, Gil and I can build a dynasty."

The guy had really fallen for Christopher's snake

oil. "Gil Christopher doesn't exactly treat his partners well," I reminded Aldo.

Aldo sneered at me. "Everything would have
been fine if my father hadn't turned on him. If he
hadn't tried to destroy the most lucrative parts of the
business that Gil was building."

Joline took a step toward Aldo, her body taut
with anger. "It was *his* company, you little brat. He
built it from the ground up. He'd created a successful, legal entity. And then that...thug...came in and
started poisoning everything. You say you're
Garland's son. But blood isn't everything. Character
is as much a part of paternity as anything. You might
have Garland's blood running through your veins,
but you don't have an ounce of his character or soul.
You're just an angry little punk who thinks the world
owes him everything because his life hasn't been
perfect. You're despicable."

Aldo's jaw tightened, a muscle ticking in his
cheek. The gun swung to center itself on my mom's
chest, and he growled a single word at her. "Die!"

"No!" I threw myself at Joline as the gun went off.
We stumbled toward the building, the world around
us exploding into light and sound. Fire seared the
flesh of my arm, but I was so drenched in adren-
aline, I barely felt it. All I knew was that it punched
me sideways, flinging me away from Joline to slam
into the cold, damp grass.

Bodies suddenly appeared from everywhere.

Aldo was on the ground and he wasn't moving. Someone was helping my mom stand. A terrified voice reached through the chaos and found me.

"Joey!" A moment later, a big, warm body dropped next to me. Strong arms reached past the agony and pulled me carefully off the grass.

I grabbed Hal's shirt and tugged it, wooziness threatening to pull me under. "My mom?"

"She's fine, honey. We need to get you to the hospital, though. You have a...splinter."

I laughed, the sound breathy and weak. "Just a..." I licked my suddenly dry lips. "Just a flesh wound." Agony sliced into my arm like it was on fire and being carved into pieces all at once. I sucked air and shuddered beneath it.

"You're going to be fine, honey," Hal whispered against my face.

His voice was husky with concern, but I drew comfort from his warmth and the solid feel of him against me. I nodded. "It's just a splinter," I said, grinning. And then I closed my eyes and let the whirlwind of light, sound, and movement carry me away.

## 19

D awn was beginning to stain the edge of the horizon beyond the window. Dressed in soft jammies and wrapped in a blanket, I stared into the fire and sipped the chamomile tea Felly had made me before she'd trudged wearily off to bed. She'd had a hard night of worry. Plus, I'd heard a rumor she might have eaten way too much ice cream.

But that was just a rumor.

My mind was still buzzing with everything that had happened. Doubt and worry and fear kept bumping up against each other in my chest, creating havoc with my nerves.

Thus the chamomile.

I wasn't nearly as confident as Felly that the tea would help. Maybe if I added a few fingers of some-thing sturdier to it...

The door closed softly behind me and Hal came

in from the cold. He slipped his cell into the pocket of his jacket. Beside me on the couch, Caphy lifted her head and gave him soft eyes, her muscular tail smacking the arm of the couch. He eyed the dog, who'd smooshed up as close to my hip as she could get and had her big head and one paw draped over my lap.

"She's not moving," I told him, feeling a grin tugging at my lips.

He sighed and sat in the chair across from the couch. "How's the arm?"

I shrugged and then regretted the movement. The wound was a shallow tear along my arm, not in any way serious, but that didn't mean it didn't hurt like the dickens. "As long as I don't move, it's fine."

Hal stared into the happily dancing fire, a haunted look on his handsome face. "You scared the stuffing out of me, Joey Fulle. I can't believe you threw yourself in front of a bullet."

I shook my head. "It wasn't a conscious decision. I just couldn't let him shoot my mom."

He sighed. "I understand the instinct to protect. I certainly get a lot of experience with that around you..."

"Har," I said, sipping my tea. "Was that Arno on the phone?"

"It was. He's still hunkered down at FBI Head-quarters with Pru." Hal shook his head. "What a mess that all is."

And my mother had been right in the middle of it. "Will they have enough to hold Gil Christopher?"

"Arno wasn't sure. They've positively identified his voice on the tape. But, as we know, no names are ever given. The recording doesn't actually tie them to the murder of that family. Pru will need to put together a case from accessory evidence."

"Dev should be able to help with that, right?" One of the first things I'd learned once I could think again was that Devon was okay. The bullet had gone through a shoulder, which would require a long recovery and lots of physical therapy, but wasn't life-threatening.

Hal nodded. "He should. Pru is also hoping to turn either Edward Johnston or Aldo." He grimaced. "I'm not hopeful about Aldo. That's one angry guy. But, with Devon's testimony, along with the evidence Garland's been collecting over the last couple of years, she's hopeful they'll be able to put together a case."

He didn't sound exactly confident. "But?" I nudged.

He glanced my way. "What?"

"I heard a giant 'But' in there."

Hal stared at his knees for a moment.

LaLee walked into the room and rubbed herself along his calves, depositing some nice cat hair on his jeans, which would send him into paroxysms of sneezing later.

As it was, he wiggled his nose and sniffed, managing to ward off a reaction for the moment.

Having done her good deed for all of catdom, the Siamese jumped up on the couch and onto the back, draping herself behind me and purring loudly.

"I'm afraid the feds did too great a job with Garland's bad boy image. The public hates him. If you ask the average man on the street about Garland Medford, the reaction is that he should be executed for his crimes. Garland better have a really good lawyer. He's going to need it."

I thought about what he said for a moment. "Maybe George Shulz has an opening on his calendar."

Shulz was a Deer Hollow lawyer...currently our only lawyer. He was also a self-proclaimed sociopath and had more cats than one human should have. Neither of those things exactly endeared him to my PI, who had a serious allergy to cats.

Hal groaned. "You probably don't want to go there."

We sat in silence for a moment, thinking. The fire was mesmerizing and, despite my roiling thoughts, the chamomile had started to work its magic. Still, I pushed weariness aside, not yet ready to go to bed.

I cocked my head at Hal. "You never told me what happened at the hotel after Joline and I were dragged away."

He grimaced at my characterization, clearly not liking it. "Garland's guys are good. They quickly regained control of the situation, contained Johnston's thugs, and called for an ambulance." He touched the swollen gash on his forehead. "Garland and I called Arno and started after you. He was certain they were taking you to the mansion, so that's where we went. But we were forced to hold outside the place while Pru tried to determine where they were keeping you." His eyes lit up. "The FBI has the coolest toys."

I laughed. "What kinds of toys?"

"They have thermal imaging sensors that can see through walls to determine where the people are. Imagine our surprise when we saw two small heat images on the top floor, kicking the stuffing out of a big guy."

I grinned. "That's really strange."

"Yeah." He shook his head, chuckling.

We fell silent again. Despite my best intentions, my body was starting to give out on me. I stifled a yawn, then shook it off.

"I wonder why Garland never embraced his son," I said, half to myself. Despite the man's flaws, and they were legion, he wasn't a cold man. I just didn't see him ignoring his own son.

"Pru did ask Garland about Aldo. Apparently, he was the result of a fling with an Italian supermodel. Garland didn't know the kid was his until recently.

Amazingly, the woman never told him he had a son. Not even when she called Garland a few months ago and asked him to give Aldo a job at Medford Industries. Once Garland was declared dead, Christopher approached Aldo and made him a lot of promises if he'd help him find that memory stick. Aldo was happy to help. Especially when Cristopher tapped into the guy's anger at Medford. He offered Aldo a partnership, a chance to replace his father at Medford Industries, and Aldo jumped at it. Then, unknown to his new partner, he apparently approached Pru and told her he was Garland's son and he wanted to help find his dad's killer."

"Devious," I said, frowning.

"Yeah. Aldo's nothing if not ambitious. I'm guessing he was going to see which side looked more promising for his future. If he could get rid of Christopher, he might have believed that, as Garland's only child, he'd inherit the company."

"Wait, he knew about Pru?"

"Christopher told him. He'd known about Garland's work with the feds ever since he helped Sasha disappear with that recording. That's why he tried to kill him. He'd just been waiting for the right moment."

"Aldo told me he'd been playing both sides," I admitted. "I hadn't realized how accurate that statement was." I thought about it for a minute. "But that whole thing with him breaking into my house and the helicopter. What was that all about? I assumed he was working with Garland. He even warned me about Pru, though that turned out to be a lie."

"A lie crafted to make you trust him, no doubt. From what I can put together, his being at your home that night was just a coincidence. They'd apparently worked their way around to believing the memory stick had to be hidden here, in the house. So, Aldo came to look for it. I'm guessing that, while they were here, they got word that there was an incoming chopper. So they retreated. That timing was good for you. I doubt their being here would have ended well."

A light bulb came on in my brain. "And then I stupidly followed them."

"And they had to stop you." Hal shook his head. "You're going to be the death of me."

"But my mom was in the house. Did he know that?"

"She wasn't here when they were. Remember, the chopper dropped her after you left. But they had to wonder who was bringing a chopper onto your property. Garland does have his own helicopter and bringing her in via the chopper probably seemed like the safest option. I'm wondering now, though, if it didn't backfire. That's probably what brought them back here the next day."

"If Aldo knew Garland was alive, why didn't he tell Gil Christopher?"

"I don't think he knew until the next day in the woods. When they ran into you and your mom and Garland rode a 4-wheeler to the rescue. Once they realized Medford was still alive, he and Christopher probably decided to pin the attack in the woods on Garland, and eventually, yours and your mom's deaths. They'd have probably gotten away with it too because everyone already believed Garland was a thug."

"And they no doubt were prepared to pin everything else on him once he was arrested."

"Yep. All they needed to do was get rid of that recording and any evidence Garland had gathered."

I thought about that for a minute, then I remembered a detail from the beginning of everything. A time that seemed like months ago after everything that had happened. "Now that we know all the players, does anybody match the description of the guy who called me on your phone at Bend Over and Coffee?"

Hal considered my question and shook his head. "I didn't see anybody matching that description among Christopher or Medford's guys."

I chalked that up to one mystery we couldn't solve. I bit back a sigh. "So, how did Aldo hook back up with Garland?"

Hal frowned. "After the attack in the woods, Garland realized he needed to beef up his security team. He contacted some guys he'd known and trusted for years, and one of them suggested they bring Aldo in too. Garland agreed, figuring Aldo was safe because he was new enough that Christopher wouldn't have gotten his hooks into him, also because of his connection to Aldo's mom, the model, who Garland *considered* a trusted friend." Hal frowned. "He was wrong."

My eyes went wide. "Wasn't Aldo's mother trustworthy?"

"She might have been, but she had blinders on where her only child was concerned. She apparently overheard Garland on the phone telling Pru she needed to recall your father's plane that night and mentioned it to Aldo just as an interesting example of Garland's work. She'd apparently always pushed the boy to take after Medford, although I don't think he knew Garland was his father until recently either. And, having no real love for Medford, Aldo was only too happy to tell Christopher what he'd learned, to buy himself some goodwill. I'm not even sure he knew what the information meant to Christopher."

I squeezed my eyes closed and shook my head. "Wait. I'm confused. Aldo and Christopher knew each other three years ago?"

"Yeah," Hal gave a bitter laugh. "Poor Garland. He was clueless. But Christopher had been looking for weak spots to exploit in Garland's life, and he'd found Gabriella, the supermodel. It wasn't hard for him to put two and two together and realize who

Aldo had to be. He apparently wasted no time in connecting with Aldo."

My heart twisted in pain for my mom. "So Garland was inadvertently the one responsible for my dad's death?"

Hal grimaced. "Technically, yeah. But Johnston's the one who killed them. Christopher's the one who told him to do it. Garland was only guilty of contacting the FBI. And he did that in an attempt to save Brent and Sasha. Not to hurt them."

Poor Garland. He'd been fond of Sasha Gardner and he'd apparently been in love with my mom, even then. Knowing that he'd accidentally betrayed them both had to be impossibly painful.

"It was a surprise to find Devon there tonight," Hal said.

I blew air through my lips. "No kidding. I'm guessing my mom finally called him? I doubt he could have found them otherwise."

"Seems likely," Hal agreed.

"Who'd have thunk old Dev could be a cop?" I said, laughing. "Or whatever he ended up being. A spy? I don't know. What a mess," I said, yawning.

"It is a mess. Though, to be fair to everybody, I don't think much of what happened was planned. Garland destroyed their original plans when he managed to survive their attempt to kill him. Christopher was good at adjusting on the fly. But your mom threw another wrench into his plans by coming back to Deer Hollow." Hal grinned. "Nobody ever said being an evil mastermind was easy."

"Nope," I managed before my jaw cracked on another wide yawn.

"Come on, sleeping beauty. Let' get you into bed. Have you taken your pain meds?"

"Not yet. They'll make me sleepy."

"Sleep is good. You need it. And when you wake up tomorrow...or today actually...we'll go see your mom, and you can clear the air. Starting today, your mom no longer needs to run and hide. Your lives are going to change again. Are you ready for that?"

I thought about his question. It would definitely take some getting used to again. I frowned, thinking of the man in my front yard, staring up at me. Had it been a dream? Maybe. But Hal had found footprints. I might never know. But I intended to talk to Joline about it. My mom had kept a lot of secrets from me. I wondered if my dad being alive was another one of those secrets.

I leaned against Hal as we trudged slowly up the stairs. Since I'd decided to go to sleep, I was suddenly beyond exhausted. "We'll figure it out," I told him. "Whatever happens, at least we'll be together again. It's all good."

"Yeah," he agreed. "It's all good. Oh, have I mentioned my parents want to come back to Deer Hollow? They thought they'd stay a couple of nights this time."

All the blood left my face, and I stumbled as I stepped onto the landing at the top of the stairs. "Oh?" I cleared my throat. "That's awesome news." It wasn't my fault my throat closed like a vise on the words so that they emerged more like the croaks of a frog than a human voice.

He gave me a strange look. "That's okay, isn't it? I thought maybe they could stay here with you. My cabin is just so small."

I stopped in my tracks and stared at him, something niggling as he frowned and cocked his head.

"What?"

I narrowed my eyes on him and he finally couldn't stand it. He laughed. "You should see your face."

I smacked him. "You're a very cruel man."

"I was just testing the, 'as long as we're together' theory. It seems to have a few holes in it."

I smacked him again. "I'm going to put a few holes in you, Hal Amity."

He wrapped himself around me, pinning my arms to my sides so I couldn't hit him again. "Such a violent woman." He kissed my forehead. "Maybe I should ask them to bring Asher too. He seemed to have a calming influence on you when he was here."

I squealed and kicked at his shins. He danced away, down the hall with me hot on his trail. Caphy brought up the rear, excited and bouncing, tongue lolling in a doggie grin. She was ready for whatever I had in mind.

I stopped when Hal ducked into my father's old office and looked down at my dog. "Here's the plan," I told her. "I'll trip him and you stick your tongue up his nose."

Caphy barked enthusiastically. She was more than happy to do her part.

Unfortunately for our best-laid plans, Hal grabbed me as soon as I stepped through the door and wrapped me in his arms. When his lips found mine, I forgot all about tripping him.

But I fully intended to give Caphy her chance at revenge as soon as I got the opportunity.

After all, revenge is a dish best served cold.

And my dog and I never missed a chance to dish it up.

The End

## ALSO BY SAM CHEEVER

If you enjoyed **Resurrected Bumpkin**, you might also enjoy these other fun mystery series by Sam. To find out more, visit the **BOOKS** page at www.samcheever.com:

Country Cousin Mysteries, f**or more fun with Joey, Hal, and Caphy!**
Gainfully Employed Mysteries
Silver Hills Cozy Mysteries
Enchanting Inquiries Paranormal Mysteries
Reluctant Familiar Paranormal Mysteries
Yesterday's Paranormal Mysteries
And More...

## READ MORE COUNTRY COUSIN MYSTERIES

If you enjoyed **Resurrected Bumpkin**, you might want to check out the rest of the series: https://samcheever.com/books/#Country

Enjoy this taste of Book 1: Humpty Bumpkin:

---

*She's just a country girl who loves her dog. But her life is about to get less countrified and more...erm...homicide.*

Deer Hollow is a small community built in a verdant, rolling countryside. The nearest big city is over an hour away and big city ways are rejected at the Hollow. Unfortunately, the big city isn't the only place where bad things can happen.

Things like murder...which has a funny way of messin' up a debutante's day and turning a sunny Sunday in June right over onto its bucolic head.

## HUMPTY BUMPKIN

The whole communication revolution thing is a mixed bag of wonderful and tedious. Things like cell phones are a revelation, allowing twenty-something women like me, who have trouble sitting still, to stay in touch with the important people in their lives while we go about our business.

But even the best innovations have their downside.

For example, a wise woman once told me never to answer a phone call whose number you don't recognize. *Answer at your own risk*, my cousin Felicity proclaimed one rainy day in the arboretum.

And I've since witnessed the intelligence of her advice. Several times over.

Unfortunately, I'm apparently a slow learner.

"Hello?"

"Is this Miss Joey Fulle?"

I frowned, not liking the "I want to sell you a bridge" tone of the caller's voice. "Nope, sorry. I think you have the wrong number."

"Actually, I believe I have the right number, Miss Fulle."

"You're not right," I said quickly and disconnected before the man on the other end of the phone had a chance to give me bad news. I had no idea what kind of bad news I was expecting. But I knew it was there, lurking like a vulture in a tree, ugly and ravenous.

I tugged the soft twisty off my shoulder length red-blonde hair and reached up to smooth the hair back into my favorite style, which was a high ponytail. Sweat dripped down between my shoulder blades and I was glad I'd dressed for the heat of an early June morning. Though my plain white tank top and cut off jean short shorts were already damp.

My dog, Cacophony, Caphy for short, bounded up and stopped in front of me, a clump of fur between her jaws. I grimaced. "Caphy, what did you do? Have you killed something again?"

A blonde pit bull with gorgeous green eyes, Caphy bounced several times, her muscular haunches springing her several inches off the ground each time, and then barked happily and ran off again, tail whipping the air. I sighed, knowing I should follow her and see if I could save whatever she'd decided to "play" with.

My phone rang again. I hit *Ignore* and trudged after my dog. "Caphy girl, where'd you go?"

The distant sound of barking drew me to a copse of old trees, their gnarled branches bigger around than I was and tangled together high overhead. It was behind one of these, an elegant old Elm tree whose knobby arms spread wider than the rest, that my dog was mostly hidden. I could see her butt wagging happily as she moved around behind the tree.

"Caphy, come!"

My sweet Pitty bounced out from behind the distant tree and grinned at me, her entire body vibrating with excitement. "What have you found, girl?" I murmured to myself. "Come on, Caphy."

But she turned back to whatever she was exploring. That was when I realized she must have cornered something. I picked up the pace and hurried in her direction.

By the time I was fifteen feet away I smelled something rotting and knew that, whatever she'd found, I wouldn't be saving it.

Real panic set in. "Caphy, you come here right now!"

My dog disappeared behind the tree and I growled with frustration. But a moment later she reappeared, heading in my direction with something hanging out of her mouth. "Ugh!" I fought an impulse to turn and run. Being corpse-woman was not tops on my list of favorite things.

In fact, I was pretty sure it wasn't on the list at all. "Drop it, Cacophony."

Of course she ignored me, her steps becoming bouncier and more excited the closer she came. Clearly she wanted to share her treasure with me. I didn't know how to impress upon her that having a mangled, half dried corpse of a bunny or squirrel dropped on my shoes didn't take me to my happy place. My usual response of shrieking and running screaming away from her treasure just didn't seem to be doing much to teach her.

She was a very bull-headed pitty. I grinned at my pun.

Caphy ran up and dropped to her haunches a few feet away. She kept hold of the object, which I was trying hard not to look at, as if she was afraid I was going to take it away from her. She would be right about that. But it wasn't going to happen until I had a bag or something to use so I didn't have to touch it. I tried one more time to get her to let loose of whatever she was clutching between her jaws. "Drop it, girl." If I was really lucky I could convince her to let go of it and I could drag her home.

To my shock she lowered her head and released the contents of her mouth.

I glanced down. My stomach did a painful little dance and my gag reflex kicked in. Caphy was watching me very carefully, letting the object lie there as if checking to see how I would react. I was glad it was out of her mouth.

In fact, I would have been elated about it.

But I was too busy shrieking and running away. It might not work for her...but it worked just fine for me.

---

Deputy Arno Willager peered toward the object hulking under the trees. Two, skinny white stick-like things protruded from one end, their bony lengths painted in red streaks. He narrowed his dark brown gaze at the thing, no doubt gawking at the enormous feet on the end of the sticks.

I shuddered beside him, my dog vibrating excitedly next to me on a leash.

"Is this your chipper, Joey?"

I gave him the full force of my hostile blue gaze. "Uh, no, Deputy Willager. It's not my chipper. And, before you ask, that's not my body either."

He lifted a golden eyebrow and quirked wide lips as he skimmed my own personal body a long, slow look. "Oh, I can see that."

I frowned but didn't scold him for giving me the once over. I was on uneven ground with that one because I was pretty sure there'd been one time at a party in high school when I'd been in a closet with

Arno, our star quarterback at the time. We'd been pretty drunk and the details of what we'd been doing in there were vague. I decided that changing the subject might be a good idea. "Do you know..." I swallowed hard. "—who it is?"

Arno wrinkled his nose. "Can't be more than a couple people around here with feet that big."

I nodded, covering my nose with a hand as a warm breeze carried the butcher shop stench in our direction. "It's horrible."

Arno didn't respond. Finally, I looked at him. "Did you call Doctor Miller?"

"I did."

"Well that's good." I glanced down at the item on the ground a few feet away. It was part of a hand. A man's hand if size was any indication. The ends of the fingers were missing, and my stomach roiled.

"Tell me how you found it."

"I told you already. "

"Humor me, Joey."

I sighed. "Caphy and I were taking a walk. It's a nice day."

He scoured me a look and I fought a grin. He was just too easy to annoy for his own good. "Caphy ran up ahead and came back with fur in her mouth."

"Fur?"

"Well...I thought it was fur. But clearly it wasn't." My gaze skimmed to the small patch of scalp resting in the dirt where Caphy had dropped it.

"Did you walk up to the chipper?"

"No."

"You didn't touch anything? Move the body parts...?"

"Ew! Of course not. Why would you even ask me that?"

"It's my job."

Frustration twanged my last nerve. Arno had always been a man of few words, but he had to know I had about a thousand questions. As if reading my mind, he turned to frown down at me. The sun dropped slowly behind him, forming a backdrop for his tall, lean frame, narrow hips and broad shoulders. Arno's face was classically handsome, with a clean-shaven square jaw, sexy brown eyes and a pleasantly-shaped mouth with a slightly fuller lower lip that was immensely appealing. Two lines rode the space between his dense golden brows as he looked at me. He was clearly chewing on something he thought he should tell me.

"What is it, Arno?"

The worry lines deepened and he held my gaze with a searching one. "You can't talk about this, Joey. This is an ongoing investigation and I need you to promise me you won't spill details around town."

"I don't know any details."

"You know more right now than anybody else except the killer." He lifted a golden brow for emphasis.

His words finally sank in. "Oh. Yikes."

"I need you to keep a low profile until we figure out what's going on."

"Surely this is someone from outside the *Hollow*."

He shrugged. "We don't know that yet."

I fell silent, chewing my bottom lip as a distant rumbling noise climbed ever closer to the spot where we stood. That would be Doctor Miller and the deputies Arno had called. They would have left their cars on the road and were approaching on all-terrain vehicles. My family's property included well over a hundred acres without roads. And the spot where Arno and I stood was in the most remote section of it all. The killer couldn't have found a more private spot to stick some poor schmoe into a wood chipper.

Finally, I nodded. "Okay. I promise."

"Good. Now you should get on home with that dog. She's disrupted the crime scene enough."

Caphy whined softly and dropped to her wide haunches, plying the deputy with a grin and soft eyes for good measure.

She wrung a grin out of him and he reached out to scratch the wide spot between her eyes. "You're a good girl, Caphy."

My pitty leapt to her feet and started wagging from her nose to the deadly whip of her tail, which unfortunately was smacking painfully against my leg.

I gave her leash a tug and, with one final look at the horror between the trees, we started back toward home. Despite my promise to keep the body in the chipper to myself, I had no intention of doing it. Whoever that poor soul was, he or she was killed on my property.

That made it personal.

And, personally, I didn't like it when people started flinging other people into wood chippers in my woods.

It was rude and disturbing.

And nipping it in the bud as quickly as possible seemed like the logical thing to do.

https://samcheever.com/books/#Country

## ABOUT SAM CHEEVER

USA Today and WSJ Bestselling Author Sam Cheever writes contemporary and paranormal mystery and suspense, creating stories that draw you in and keep you eagerly turning pages. Known for writing great characters, snappy dialogue, and unique and exhilarating stories, Sam is the award-winning author of 80+ books.

To learn more about Sam and her work, visit her at one of her online hotspots:
www.samcheever.com
samcheever@samcheever.com